5

D1491353

SWEET HISTORY

NICOLE ELLIS

1

$\mathcal{T}$he Donohue Gallery in Seattle was packed with people and Charlotte suddenly felt self-conscious. Although her painting was but one of many at the show, there were people checking it out and commenting on her use of color. This was good though, right? This was what she'd always wanted. She hovered near the wall, not wanting to miss anything, but not wanting to join the crowd either.

"Charlotte, I want you to meet some of our patrons." Raymond Donohue appeared beside her, cupping her elbow to guide her over to a well-dressed couple in their fifties. Her stomach churned. This show had the power to make or break her career as an artist.

"Dana, Chet, this is Charlotte Gray, the up-and-coming artist I told you about." He gestured to one of her paintings hanging on the wall. "This is one of her newest pieces."

All of them stopped to assess the painting. Charlotte held her breath as the woman sipped thoughtfully from the half-full glass of white wine she held in the crook of her index finger. Finally, she nodded in approval. "It's beautiful."

Charlotte's chest puffed up a little and she smiled at the woman. "Thank you."

The watercolor of Candle Beach at sunset was one of her favorites. She'd begun painting it on a beautiful summer evening from a perch along the cliff, high above the sand and water. It had taken some time, but she'd managed to capture the moment when the sky filled with a rich gold that melted into brilliant hues of purple and rose.

"Are there more?" The man glanced at his wife, who nodded.

Charlotte was about to speak, but Raymond cut in first. "She's going to have her own solo show in a few weeks and you'll be able to see the full collection then. I'll call you with the details once we get them worked out."

"Ah." The man smiled at Charlotte. "We'll be sure to come back for that showing."

They walked away, with Raymond close on their heels. He looked over his shoulder at Charlotte and gave her an encouraging smile.

She wanted to squeal and jump up and down, right there on the gallery floor, but restrained herself. That is, until she made it into the bathroom. She glanced at her reflection in the mirror. Her wavy blonde hair was up in a dignified bun and her mascara-accented, cornflower-blue eyes were wide with excitement. She checked under the door of the bathroom stalls for feet. They were empty, so she leaned against the counter and allowed herself one squeal.

A solo show? It was something she'd dreamed of since she first started painting, but thought would never happen. From the elegant patrons, to the delicious hors d'oeuvres, to the impressive artwork and the artists themselves, it was as though she was in some sort of fairy tale. She gave herself a quick pinch on the arm to make sure she wasn't going to wake up and find out that none of it had actually happened.

The telltale sound of high heels clicked in the hallway outside the restrooms and neared the door, so she quickly composed herself. A tall woman that Charlotte recognized as someone who worked in the gallery gave her a curt nod. Charlotte smiled as she brushed past her and out the door.

After the showing, Raymond took her aside.

"People were raving about your paintings. I think your career is going to go far."

She looked up at him. "You really think so?"

He nodded. "Yes. Your work shows much promise." He checked his watch. "I've got to finish up here, but I'll give you a call next week, and we can set up a showing of your other work."

She tried to keep it together, but excitement bubbled out of her voice. "Thank you so much for this opportunity." She calmed herself to a more professional level. "I look forward to hearing from you next week."

"Great, I'll talk to you then." He walked off toward one of the galleries.

Although it wasn't really in her budget, she'd booked a hotel nearby to stay at so that she didn't have to make the four-hour drive back to Candle Beach so late at night. She gathered her belongings from where she'd stored them in a back office of the gallery and walked the few blocks over to her hotel. Unlike back home where almost everything shut down by ten o'clock, here the city was still alive with people, flashing lights and a curious array of odors. She certainly wasn't in Candle Beach anymore.

In the hotel room, she stepped out of the black cocktail-length dress she'd had since she was in college and hung it up in the closet. When the dress was off, the magic and adrenaline of the evening wore off with it and she realized how much the experience had drained her. She retrieved her favorite pink flannel pajamas from her suitcase and eased into them, the cats imprinted on the fabric smiling at her as she pulled them over her legs. Ah. They were comfortably familiar and warm in the cool air of the hotel room.

She stood in front of the hotel mirror and stared at her reflection as she had earlier at the gallery. While she'd looked put-together before, now she was a mess. Her blonde hair had come out of the bun and the extra mascara and eye shadow she'd worn for the show had smudged around her eyes. She scrubbed the makeup off of her face until her cheeks were naturally pink. When she finished, she was just Charlotte, not some artist eager to prove her worth in a competitive world.

She flopped down on the bed, but her brain wouldn't stop spinning. In the distance, a car alarm honked incessantly until it finally shut off a few minutes later. The pillow-top mattress had appeared comfortable and inviting, but in reality, a rock would have been softer. She tossed and turned, drifting in and out of sleep until four in the morning when she called it quits.

The news about the art show was too exciting to keep to herself and she wanted to go back home to share it with her friends. She threw her clothes back in her suitcase in a haphazard fashion, not even bothering to fold the dress she'd worn the night before, and rolled the luggage down to her car, which was parked in the underground parking garage. The bill had been paid the day before, so she was free to leave whenever she wanted.

When her hands were on the steering wheel, a wide smile spread across her face. Everything she'd ever wanted in her life was coming true. An art gallery wanted her paintings for a show, she had a great group of friends, and she owned a cute little shop, Whimsical Delights.

The world around her froze. The shop. Would she be able to paint and manage the shop? Whimsical Delights was a full-time job and a half, and she'd worked hard to make it a success. If her art career took off, how would she do both?

A twinge of anxiety settled in her stomach. Ever since she'd received the call from Raymond informing her that they were interested in showing her work, she'd been on cloud nine and had worked full steam ahead to get ready for the show. She hadn't stopped to think how the increased demands on her time would affect everything else in her life on a long-term basis if the show was successful.

The air in the car seemed thinner and she opened the windows but only succeeded in breathing in a mouthful of exhaust from the diesel bus in front of her. Quickly, she closed it and turned up the fan speed for the air conditioner.

Doubt flooded over her like a rogue wave, drenching the elation she'd experienced at the art show. Was she doing the right thing? What if she couldn't manage the shop and be a serious artist at the same time? Painting in her spare time wasn't going to be enough to make it in the art world. She would be lucky to finish a few paintings a year at the level she was able to devote to it.

Her fingers tightened over the wheel as her car drove seemingly on autopilot toward Candle Beach. By the time she neared Haven Shores, a town about twenty miles from home where she'd grown up, she had worked herself into such a lather that she was lucky to notice that the needle on her gas tank was hovering just above empty. Not enough fuel to make it the rest of the way home. She exited the highway in Haven Shores, taking the turn onto Gull Street and pulling into the gas station she'd gone to hundreds of times since earning her driver's license on her sixteenth birthday.

While pumping gas into the car, she was struck with a realization. What would her parents think of her if she gave up on her dream of owning Whimsical Delights? They'd called her dreams silly and she'd fought with them over it when they wanted her to join the family real estate business after college. She'd acquiesced to their demands and become an administrative assistant at Gray & Associates Real Estate, but only for a few years while she built up enough savings to purchase inventory for her shop and the Airstream trailer that housed it.

Her gaze shifted toward the direction of her parents' house, situated on several acres on the long canal that ran through town. They'd found success in real estate, but unlike her brothers, it had never been her dream. She'd always wanted to pursue her art and run her own business. But now that she had it all, could she keep it? Had her parents been right all along? Were her dreams foolish?

She replaced the gas cap and got back into her car in a daze. *You can't do this to yourself.*

She had no idea what the future held and it seemed silly to worry about having too much going on when it hadn't even happened yet. She'd be lucky if her art career ever took off. With that thought, she lowered the window and breathed in the fresh ocean air as she drove back to Candle Beach.

Thirty minutes later, she entered town, passing through the one stoplight and waving to several people walking along Main Street that she knew. The mayor's wife Marsha and one of her friends, another one of the Ladies of Candle Beach, were power-walking down the sidewalk holding togo cups of coffee. Charlotte's friend Maggie was outside of the Bluebonnet Café clearing dishes from the breakfast rush, but she didn't see her pass by, which was probably good, or she'd be tempted to stop and block traffic to tell Maggie about the show. She parked in the small parking lot across from her apartment over To Be Read, the town's bookstore, and turned off the engine.

Saturday was usually the busiest day of the week and she needed to open Whimsical Delights soon to take advantage of the increasing tourist traffic as summer approached. First though, she needed a quick shower. After unloading her medium-sized suitcase from the trunk, she entered the bookstore's back room through the alley.

"Char?" a woman's voice called out from the adjoining office. "Is that you?"

She left her suitcase behind and poked her head into Dahlia's office.

"Hey." Charlotte pushed her hair back from her face and smiled at her friend.

Dahlia grinned at her. "Hey, yourself. How was the art show? Was it everything you dreamed it would be?"

Charlotte sighed dramatically. "It was amazing. Better than I dreamed." All of the feelings she'd had the night before reappeared. "They want to sign me for a solo show."

Dahlia's eyebrows lifted and she stood. "Really?"

Charlotte nodded. "Uh-huh."

"I'm so happy for you—and a little jealous. I wish I was as talented of a painter as you are." She walked over to Charlotte and gave her a hug. "Did they say when? I'm sure all of us would love to go." She frowned slightly. "I hope it's not after Garrett and I leave for Europe."

Charlotte laughed. "I don't know when it will be. We didn't make any definite plans." She crossed her fingers in front of her for good luck, then checked her silver wristwatch. "With any luck, the gallery owner won't change his mind. I'd better get showered if I want to open the shop on time."

Dahlia waved her hand in the air dismissively. "Of course. Go. But the other girls and I will want to hear all about it. Maybe we can meet up at Off the Vine in the next day or so?"

"I'd love that." Charlotte picked up her suitcase and opened the door to the apartment stairs. "See you later."

"See you." Dahlia went back into her office and Charlotte walked up the stairs with the heavy suitcase, dragging it by the time she reached the top step.

She'd left a window open before leaving for Seattle the morning before, and fresh air streamed through the kitchen and living room, bringing with it the scent of the roses Dahlia had planted outside the bookstore. Not for the first time, she found herself thankful that she'd moved to Candle Beach. It was close enough that she could still see her family in Haven Shores when she wanted to, but far enough away that it wasn't a daily occurrence. As the baby of the family, they'd coddled her, and it had taken her far too long to figure out her own place in the world. Here, she'd been able to make her own way, out of the shadow of her family's prominent real estate firm.

After the long drive back home and lack of sleep the night before, exhaustion hit her the moment she entered her apartment. It was still only nine o'clock in the morning and business wouldn't pick up until the afternoon, so she gave herself a few hours to take a nap. When she woke up, she showered and dressed quickly, eager to get to the shop.

While in Seattle the day before, she'd talked to a few merchants at Pike Place Market about the possibility of selling their wares in her shop. The tourists loved anything handmade locally and she liked to keep a good mix of gifts in her inventory. That was one of the things she enjoyed most about being a small business owner—sourcing the products she sold and finding things that would delight her customers—hence the name Whimsical Delights.

She hurried down the sidewalk and over a block to the empty lot where her Airstream was parked. Whenever she saw the shiny silver trailer, the fairy lights she'd strung across the parking lot and the neat white fence that bordered the lot, she was struck at how perfect the setting was. When she rounded the corner, she smiled in anticipation. Sales should be good on this sunny Saturday.

Horror quickly replaced happiness.

In her cute little lot, next to her beautiful, meticulously restored trailer, was a towering hunk of metal on wheels. What was that thing? She hurried up to it, stopping near the front of it, which bore a sign reading *Beachside BBQ.*

A food truck? What was a food truck doing next to her shop?

2

"So, what do you think, Pops?" Luke Tisdale waited with bated breath as his grandfather ran his eyes over the exterior of the Beachside BBQ food truck. He'd had the truck freshly washed and the sign painted before moving it to Candle Beach earlier that Friday morning, and he hoped it would be met with approval.

Finally, Pops looked back at him. "I'm glad you're back in the area, but this seems like a big jump from your job at that tech company in San Francisco." He peered at Luke with eyes full of kindness mixed with concern. "Are you sure this is what you want?"

Luke smiled. "Yes. I've been shadowing a guy for the last six months who owns the best barbecue food truck in the Bay Area." He shook his head. "I couldn't take working at LinkinTechno anymore."

He'd worked at the company for over seven years and while he'd learned a lot, it had been seven of the worst years of his life. He'd had very little free time and the stress of working at a start-up had been overwhelming. When they put the company up for IPO, he cashed out his shares, leaving him with more money than he'd ever dreamed possible.

Pops ran his hand reverently along the line of rivets holding the arm of the open overhang to the smooth aluminum siding. "It's a beauty." He looked directly at Luke. "But you always hated the restaurant business when you were a kid. I was surprised when you said that you intended to buy a food truck."

"I know. I think it's in my blood though. When I was trying to figure out what I wanted to do next, it was all I could think about." Luke was quiet for a moment as he folded down the steps to the back door. His grandparents had taken him and his twin sister Zoe in as toddlers after their parents died in a car accident. They'd owned a drive-in burger place nearby in Haven Shores that had been their pride and joy, but also kept them extremely busy. After Luke's grandmother died five years ago, Pops had sold it and moved into a retirement community near the water, saying the restaurant and the house he'd lived in with Grams had contained too many memories of her.

"Your grandmother was so excited when you got that scholarship to Stanford, and even more so when you landed a job at that big tech company down there. We wanted you to have more in life than living in a small town forever, running a restaurant." He looked over toward Candle Beach's small downtown area. "This is even smaller than Haven Shores. It must be a big change from living in the city."

"It is, but I think I'm going to like it a lot." Luke stuck his key in the lock of the food truck's door and jiggled it until it turned. The door squeaked and the scent of lemon cleanser from his cleaning spree the day before hit him as soon as he opened it fully.

"Okay then. If you're sure." Pops didn't look certain.

"I am. I've tried the big-city life and I'm ready for something different."

As one of the top software developers at LinkinTechno, he'd earned a great salary, but that had come with its negative aspects too. While in high school and college he'd been an awkward, skinny kid with only a few friends, but that had all changed when he started to earn more money and spent some time at the gym.

Suddenly, women had flocked to him. It had been exciting at first, but after a while, he wondered whether they were interested in him or his money. When his last girlfriend had openly announced that she was leaving him for someone making even more money than he did, he'd realized they'd probably all been gold diggers.

As a food truck owner, no one would know he was a multimillionaire. He was just another guy pursuing his passion and trying to make ends meet. Now, the next time a woman was interested in him, he'd know if it was for him or his money. Not that he expected—or wanted—a woman in his life at the moment.

"What's all of this next door?" Pops asked as he turned to survey the knickknack shop located in a vintage Airstream trailer about ten feet away. "Whimsical Delights? That doesn't seem to fit with your food truck."

Luke glanced at the other half of the lot. The shop's owner had strung up along the adjoining fence a bunch of small white lights that reminded him of Christmas lights. Although the trailer door was closed, colorful signs and stone fountains were stored outside. A rustic sign with rustic flaking white paint read *Whimsical Delights*.

What kind of name was that anyway? It was such a cutesy place that it was probably owned by a bubbly woman that he wouldn't be able to stand. He had a sinking feeling that sharing the space with the Airstream wasn't going to be all fun and games.

Surprisingly, or maybe not, he hadn't yet met the owner. When he parked the truck in the lot earlier that morning, she hadn't been there. Even though Saturdays must be a big day for tourist traffic, she still hadn't arrived yet. It was pretty obvious she didn't care about her business too much.

Luke shrugged. "I don't think it'll be there much longer." The landlord for the lot had told him that the Airstream's lease was up soon and he didn't think the owner would be staying. "Do you want to see the inside?" He jutted his thumb at the interior of the food truck.

"I wouldn't miss it," Pops said. He held on to the small grab bar at the top of the steps Luke had folded out and pulled himself up. For a man in his eighties, he was surprisingly spry.

"So, this is where the magic happens." Pops appraised the kitchen setup. His fuzzy gray hair stuck out in tufts as he bent down and opened cabinet doors to peer inside.

"Yep. I've got a four-burner stove over there, the cash register will go next to the roll-up window, and my smoker is right back there." Luke pointed through the window over the stove at a mid-sized smoker he'd pushed against the back of the lot.

Pops nodded. "It's nice. Compact, but you can get a lot done in here. It's similar to the kitchen we had at the drive-in."

While what he was saying was polite and complimentary, Luke detected a note of hesitation in his grandfather's demeanor.

"You're worried, aren't you?" He stared into Pops' face.

"I'm not worried about whether you'll succeed or not," Pops said slowly. "I'm just concerned that you'll regret this. How easy is it to get back into your career if you decide this isn't what you want?"

Luke waved his hand in the air dismissively. "They'll take me back. A really good software engineer is hard to find, and I'm one of the best. Besides, I have more than enough money to live on, even if I never worked another day in my life." He met his grandfather's gaze. "But this is what I want. I've been planning this for almost a year."

Much like any project he undertook, he'd done his homework—shadowing the owner of a popular barbecue food truck in the city, taking culinary classes to hone his skills and studying the market to determine if the concept was viable somewhere on the Washington coast. Although he'd probably never make anywhere close to what he'd made as a software developer, he was confident he could earn a decent living in this tourist town with the food truck.

It didn't really matter though. Other than his pride, failing in business wouldn't hurt his bank account. If that happened, he'd move on to the next project.

"All right. You know, I think your grandmother always hoped you and Zoe would move back to the coast and settle down here."

"I know she did." Guilt washed over him. "I'm sorry I didn't get up here that much over the last few years before she passed."

"Don't worry about it. We both knew that you and your sister had your own lives to live." He shot Luke a sly look. "But maybe you'll meet a local girl now that you're back and make this your home. That wouldn't be so bad, right? You know, I was just about your age when I met your grand-mother." A far-off expression appeared on his wizened face.

Luke stifled a grin. What were the chances he'd meet the girl of his dreams here when he'd struck out with love in a much bigger city?

"Maybe." He changed the subject. "How are things going at the retirement home?"

Pops brightened. "Good. Me and a few other guys play poker every week in the main lounge. Sometimes we even sneak in cigars if they don't catch us. The staff is pretty nice. Even though we all have kitchens in our apartments, they make cookies and stuff to serve with coffee every afternoon." He patted his pudgy belly. "I've put on a few pounds since moving in there."

"I'm glad you like it." Luke had often wondered if Pops was putting on a brave face whenever they saw each other, but he genuinely seemed to enjoy living in the retirement home. He looked at him with curiosity. "Do you miss Grams?"

Pops sighed and gazed out the window. "Every day. That woman drove me crazy sometimes, but she was the love of my life."

"It must be tough without her." Luke remembered how his grandparents would always kiss each other goodbye and how his grandmother had insisted that no one in the family ever went to bed mad at each other. There had been some tough times when it came to applying that to his relation-ship with his sister when they were teenagers, but it had always been helpful in the long run.

"It is." Pops looked down at his feet, then back up at him. "But I'm still here and I know she'd want me to try to be happy, so that's what I do, every day."

Luke nodded. "She always wanted the best for all of us."

"She did." Pops walked toward the back door. "It doesn't look like you're open for business though, and I'm starving. What is there to eat around here?"

Luke laughed. "I've heard good things about the Bluebonnet Café. Parker swears by it."

"How is Parker doing anyway? I remember how you two were always together as kids, playing in the tree house out back with your GI Joes. I heard he went into real estate like his parents. Probably making a killing on commissions with the home prices these days." He shook his head, as if thinking about how things had changed since he was young.

"Actually, he's living here in Candle Beach. He's engaged to a woman he met through work who's from here, and they've formed their own real estate company." He grinned. "I never thought I'd see Parker settle down, but he seems like he's coming into his own here."

"Ah. Is that how you found this space?" Pops looked out the open door. "It seems like a good location. Not much parking, but should be decent foot traffic." He assessed it with the keen eye of a restaurateur.

"Nope, it wasn't one of Parker's listings. I checked out a few of his properties, but I saw an ad for this space in the local paper. I called the owner and worked everything out with him."

"Well, your truck looks good here. I'm proud of you," Pops said gruffly with a slight gleam in his eyes.

"Thanks." Luke reached out instinctively and hugged the old man.

They exited the food truck and he locked the door before they left for an early lunch. Having his grandfather here made everything seem so real. He'd been planning this move for such a long time that now that it was actually happening, it seemed crazy. Had he really quit a high-paying job for this?

He breathed in the salt air that always reminded him of home and glanced at his grandfather. Besides his twin sister, Pops was the only family member he had left. Yep. Moving to Candle Beach was worth any sacrifices he'd made.

3

*A*ny thoughts about the weather or potential sales flew out of Charlotte's head the moment she saw the food truck. She froze in place, her eyes scouring the side of the truck. Beachside BBQ? Her stomach grumbled involuntarily at the thought of barbecue, reminding her that she'd skipped breakfast.

Barbecue was all fine and good, but it didn't belong two feet away from her shop. She forced herself to move her feet toward the truck. A small sign on the closed-up front window announced that the truck would be open for business for lunch on Monday. At least that was a small piece of good fortune.

How could her landlord have allowed a food truck to share her space? She vaguely remembered something about being told that the piece of property she'd parked her trailer on was only half of the space, but she'd assumed if the landlord eventually rented it out it would be to another retail store, not a fast food truck. And she should have been consulted first if that wasn't the case.

Something inside the truck made a noise, startling her.

Someone was in there. She narrowed her eyes and marched around to the back door of the truck, rapping on the small covered window.

"Hold on," a man's deep voice said. "I'll be there in a minute."

She stopped knocking and stood in front of the door, her fists balling up at her sides. This wasn't going to be a pleasant conversation. There was no way he could have his food truck there. The only answer was for him to move to a different site.

Where that would be, she didn't know, but it wasn't her problem. This was a prime spot in Candle Beach's small downtown, perfect for catching the tourists as they came and went from the beach—exactly the reason she'd chosen it for herself.

The door creaked open and from behind it, the man said, "Sorry, I was finishing up some inventory. Did you need something?"

He opened the door completely and she took a step back. He crinkled up his face and glanced back into the truck, as though just remembering something. His hesitation gave her a chance to look at him more closely.

That can't be who I think it is.

He was tall, with a runner's physique and a face that she'd normally find attractive. Thick brown hair flopped over his forehead and he brushed it back, then finally looked directly at her.

His eyes widened. "Chatty Charlie? Is that you?"

She opened and shut her mouth like a demented fish. Chatty Charlie. Now that was a nickname she hadn't heard in many years. The only people to call her that were her older brother Parker and his best friend Luke. The non-affectionate nickname had stemmed from their belief that she and her friends did nothing but shop and gab together all the time.

Unfortunately, they'd been right. It hadn't been until she was a freshman in college, away from her parents, that she'd realized what a privileged life she'd led. Ever since, she'd taken steps to not be that person. She took a deep breath.

Get it together, Charlotte. You're not Chatty Charlie anymore.

"It's Charlotte actually." She pressed her lips together and breathed calmly through her nose.

He looked as though he were trying to hide a smile. "Of course. Charlotte. It's nice to see you again. I didn't realize you lived around here."

She peered at him, unsmiling. "Parker never said anything about you coming back to the area." The last she'd heard, Luke was working in San Francisco at some startup company as a hotshot computer programmer. Her brother had mentioned something about going down there to see him about a year ago, but that was all she'd heard about it. Certainly, there had been no mention of Luke moving to Candle Beach.

Luke shrugged. "He's been so busy with Gretchen and their new company. I'd been looking for the perfect spot for my new food truck up and down the West Coast and when I came upon this spot here, I snapped it up." He looked around the lot appraisingly. "It's good to be home."

She clenched her jaw. "It is a nice spot—for my shop. Look, I'm sorry, but you can't have your food truck here. I can't have people shopping with barbecue smoke drifting through my trailer."

He cocked his head to the side. "I don't think it's up to you. I signed a year-long lease with the landlord and I intend to stay here."

Her heart hammered. She was stuck with Luke as a

neighbor for an entire year, if not longer? A food truck next door was bad enough, but why did it have to be Luke's food truck?

He'd always treated her like an annoying little sister and it didn't seem like that had changed one bit in the twelve years since she'd last seen him. There had to be some way of getting him to leave.

"Why are you here anyway? Did you lose your job?" She cringed inwardly at her hostility, but the question had come out before she could rethink it.

He clenched his jaw. "No. I chose to buy the food truck and make this my new career. As you know, I grew up at my grandparents' drive-in, so I'm familiar with the business."

"That's great, and I'm sure there are plenty of other places for you to park your truck." She didn't know of any, but there had to be something.

"But I have a perfectly good space. You could move your business elsewhere. As you said, there has to be other places if you feel like you can't share the space with me."

"I can't afford to do that." She'd invested everything in her business. Although she worked hard, there was still only a small amount over what was required to pay for the basics in her bank account. Moving would put a serious dent in the small savings she had.

"Right ..." he drawled. "A Gray not able to afford something? Can't you ask your parents for a loan if it's that big of a deal? I remember that's how it used to work for you and your siblings in high school."

She stared at him in shock as all of the memories and shame about how she'd acted back then socked her in the gut. A gust of wind blew her hair into her face and she pushed it back behind her ears, not caring how she looked.

"This isn't going to work. You'll have to find something

else." She turned on her heels and stalked off to the Airstream's door. As she stood on the three-foot-square wooden deck she'd built to make entry into the trailer easier for customers, she snuck a peek back at him. He was leaning against the truck with his arms folded across his chest, a bemused expression on his face.

She averted her eyes before he could see her staring, quickly pulled the door open and entered the trailer. Usually she loved sitting on her padded, high-back stool near the entrance, working at the tiny desk she used as a counter. From there, she could see the customers shopping the larger merchandise she kept outside and still work on all of the paperwork that came with owning a small business.

But not today. Today she had a hard time focusing on her business because of Luke. Once, she saw him start to come over to her trailer, but a customer appeared and he turned back around. He'd been standoffish when he was Parker's best friend in high school and that trait had obviously evolved into full-on rudeness. Not that she'd been overly polite in her exchange with him either.

A woman walked up to the Airstream and toured it, then approached Charlotte. "I love your shop. I told all of my friends about how cute it is."

"Thanks." Charlotte smiled at her. "Is there anything I can help you find?"

"Oh no, I think I'm just going to get this today." She held out a pair of frog earrings. "My daughter loves frogs and I wanted to get her a souvenir of our trip to the beach."

"Great." Charlotte took the earrings from her, rang them up and then wrapped them in tissue paper. Then she put the package into a small gift bag stamped with her store name and handed it to the woman.

"Thank you." The woman hesitated. "Do you know

when that barbecue place is opening? I don't remember seeing it before."

"I think it might open on Monday." Charlotte tried to hide her displeasure.

"Oh, I hope so. We're leaving Tuesday afternoon. I hope it opens while we're still here. My husband loves barbecue."

Charlotte forced a smile and pointed at the truck. "The owner is there if you'd like to ask him."

The woman beamed back at her. "Thank you. I think I will. I hope you have a nice day."

"You too," Charlotte answered.

The customer walked down the steps and across the lot to the food truck.

Charlotte hung back, watching as she approached the truck and knocked on the door. Luke stepped out and spoke with the woman. His eyes darted to Charlotte and then refocused on the woman in front of him. The customer left smiling, so she must have received a satisfactory response from him.

"Charlotte," he called out when the woman was gone.

She didn't look at him. She hadn't much liked the geeky Luke she'd known before because of how he and her brother treated her, but this arrogant jerk was even worse. There had to be some way to get rid of him and his food truck, because she couldn't see them ever becoming friendly.

4

*L*uke walked into To Be Read and scanned the bookstore for the entrance to Charlotte's apartment. After their meeting earlier that day, he'd felt bad about what he'd said to her. He never should have implied that her parents were funding her business, but she'd really gotten his goat with her demands that he move out of the space. He'd called Parker once he was done getting things ready in the food truck and he'd told him that she lived in an apartment over the bookstore.

"Can I help you?" a woman asked. "Are you looking for something in particular?"

"Not something, but someone," he said. "I was hoping to talk to Charlotte, and her brother said to come here."

"How do you know Charlotte?" She peered at him keenly, as though trying to figure out if he was friend or foe.

"I grew up with her. Parker and I are best friends and I've recently moved back to town."

"Ah. You must be Luke. Gretchen mentioned you were moving here." She beamed at him. "I'm Dahlia. This is my bookstore." She held out her hand to shake.

"I am Luke." He smiled at her and took her hand. "Nice to meet you too."

"Come with me. I'll show you where Charlotte's apartment is." She led him through a door into a back room and pointed at the open stairs. "She must be home because the bottom door is open. She usually shuts it when she isn't here." She turned to leave. "Let me know if you need anything."

"I will. Thank you," he called after her. Then, he eyed the stairs. Dahlia had assumed that he and Charlotte were friends, but after their exchange earlier, he didn't think he could call the relationship between them friendly. With any luck, he'd be able to change that with this visit.

He tromped up the stairs and knocked at the closed door at the top.

"It's unlocked," Charlotte called out.

He entered a small living room and kitchen, where Charlotte was stirring something on the stove top. Whatever it was smelled wonderful, with aromas of garlic, onion and some sort of meat. Somehow though, he didn't think he'd be getting an invitation to stay for dinner.

She stirred the pot once more, set the wooden spoon down on the counter and turned to face him.

"Oh. It's you."

He stuck his hands in his pockets. "Yeah, sorry."

She crossed her arms over her chest. "I thought you were Dahlia."

"She let me in and told me where I could find you."

"I'm going to have to talk with her about letting strangers in," she grumbled.

"Don't be mad at her. I told her we knew each other from when we were kids and that I was Parker's friend. She just assumed that you and I were friends too."

"We're not."

"I know." He took a deep breath. "I'm really sorry about what I said earlier. It was wrong of me to make any assumptions about how you run your business, and I understand why you're upset about me moving my food truck onto the same lot as your shop."

"Uh-huh." She removed a pitcher of water from the fridge and refilled a glass on the table, then sat down in one of the two seats. Although it was warm in the apartment, she didn't offer him anything.

He sat down across from her anyway.

"I really am sorry. But there's nothing I can do about it. I signed a lease already. And if it wasn't me moving in there, it would be someone else."

She eyed him. "Another retail shop would be fine. It's the barbecued food—and you—that I object to."

He pushed his chair back, accidentally bumping the table with his too-long legs. The table shook violently, causing the full glass of water to wobble too. He managed to catch it before it fell off the table, but not before it tipped fully on its side, spilling the contents over the edge of the table, directly into Charlotte's lap.

She gasped and jumped up when the icy water hit her. "Seriously?"

All he could do was stare at her, still holding the empty glass. "I'm so sorry."

She looked down at her lemon-yellow t-shirt and jeans that were now completely soaked.

"Let me help you." He grabbed a dish towel off of the oven door and moved toward her.

She held her hands in the air. "I need to change."

He mopped up the water and wrung out the dish towel in the sink, setting the wet cloth next to it on the counter.

He'd cleaned up the mess, but now what? This apology wasn't going so well.

She was still ensconced in her bedroom with the door tightly shut, but paintings leaning against the living room walls caught his eye. He moved closer to examine them. Most of them were outdoor scenes of places he recognized in the area. She was a talented artist. Any of them were pieces he'd love to have in his own home. An easel was set up in the corner, with an unfinished canvas on it.

"What are you doing?" she asked as she opened the door and caught him checking out her art.

"Did you paint all of these? They're beautiful," he said in response.

Her expression softened. "Yes, they're mine. But why are you still here after drenching me?"

"I didn't get a chance to apologize for that—or to make you understand that I didn't mean what I said earlier. If we're going to share that space, we need to at least have an amicable relationship."

"We're not friends," she said stubbornly.

"I know." He moved around an end table that was covered in unopened mail. "But Parker's my best friend and you're his sister, so for his sake, let's call a truce, okay?"

"Fine." She spun around and hurried to the stove. "My stew is going to burn. You can see yourself out."

He opened the apartment door and an orange and white cat flew past him down the stairs and through the open door at the bottom. Where had he come from? He had a bad feeling about this.

"Uh, Charlotte?"

"You're still here?" she said without turning around.

"Do you have a cat?"

She whipped around. "Yes, Alistair." She scanned the

room frantically and narrowed her eyes at him. "Did you let him out?"

"Maybe?" He winced. Yeah, this wasn't good. "He came out of nowhere and took off down the stairs."

"And you didn't stop him?" She flicked the burner off and pushed past him.

"Alistair! Alistair!" she called out. "Dahlia's not going to be happy if he's loose in the bookstore. She let me adopt him from the Humane Society and have him here, but she's not keen on him being in the store."

"I'm so sorry," he said helplessly as he followed her down the stairs to the storeroom. "I think I heard something in there." He pointed to a half-open door.

Charlotte rushed over to the door and pushed it open slowly. She flipped on a light, revealing a small bathroom. A pitiful meow came from inside.

"Alistair?" she called softly. "It's just me." She went inside and shut the door on Luke. A minute later, she emerged with a ball of fluff pressed tightly against her chest. "Thank goodness you didn't leave the back door open too. He's still a little jumpy, which is why he ran when you opened the door."

"I really am sorry." He felt like he'd been saying that a lot lately.

She moved toward the stairs. "I know. You said that already." She stroked Alistair's fur and then walked up the stairs, calling over her shoulder, "Please make sure to shut the door on your way out."

He sighed. He'd come here to fix things with Charlotte and he'd made things ten times worse. At this rate, she'd never forgive him.

5

"*C*hatty Charlie?" Maggie raised her eyebrows. She pressed her lips together as if struggling not to laugh, then raised her glass to take a sip of red wine.

Gretchen had no such qualms. She immediately burst out into laughter.

Charlotte fixed her eyes on her friend and Gretchen quieted. It was a Friday night and Off the Vine was close to capacity, but the three of them had managed to find a small table in a corner of the wine bar. A jazz quartet had set up across the room, but they hadn't started playing yet.

"I'm sorry, I can't help it. That's hilarious. Parker never mentioned calling you that." She grabbed a tortilla chip and dipped it into the creamy crab and artichoke dip.

"It is not." Charlotte pouted. She'd grown up hearing Parker and Luke calling her that nickname. "I hate being called that."

All around them, people chattered, but Charlotte couldn't focus on anything other than Luke Tisdale. The man was infuriating. She hadn't seen him in twelve years and he still saw her as a ditzy teenager.

Maggie reached across the table and patted Charlotte's hand. "We're sorry we laughed, right Gretchen?" She stared pointedly at their friend.

"No, not really."

Now it was Charlotte's turn to glare at Gretchen.

"Look, high school was so long ago. I'm sure both of you have changed," Gretchen said as she reached for a stuffed mushroom cap. "He doesn't still think of you as Chatty Charlie." She fought to not laugh again and peered at Charlotte. "Why did he call you that anyway? Were you a really annoying chatterbox when you were a kid?"

Charlotte squirmed. "I'm sure I annoyed my brother and Luke, but they called me that because they thought all I ever did was talk and shop." She took a sip of her wine and her lips puckered at the initial sourness. "I may have been slightly spoiled by my parents. In my defense, all of my friends were like that too." It made her a little sick now to think about how entitled she'd been as a teenager. She leaned back. "But now that's the only way Luke will ever see me."

"Do you want him to see you another way?" Maggie asked, her eyes wide with feigned innocence. Beside her, Gretchen chortled.

"No, no, that's not what I meant! I don't see him as anything but my brother's annoying friend." Charlotte felt her face flame and fumbled for the correct thing to say. "Ugh. I'm not interested in him like that." He'd been nothing but a thorn in her side since she'd found his food truck in her lot last week. It had been bad enough having that monstrous truck next to her shop, but once he'd fired up the smoker and began serving customers, things had gotten worse.

Still, she couldn't help but remember how his skinny

face and body had filled out since high school. While he'd been pretty nerdy then, any woman would find him attractive now. Correction—any woman but her.

"Uh-huh," Gretchen said dryly. "I've met Luke. Parker and I had him over for dinner a few nights ago." She turned to Maggie. "He's not hard on the eyes."

"You were just complaining to us that there weren't many available men in town. Maybe this is fate." Maggie grinned at Charlotte.

Charlotte's skin crawled at Maggie's suggestion. If having Luke reappear after all these years to laugh at her and ruin her business was fate, the world must hate her.

She shook her head. "Nope, I'm swearing off men. I don't have time for dating right now. There's too much going on in my life. Besides, Luke Tisdale is the last person I'd ever want to be with." She shuddered. Her brother's friend? Seriously?

Maggie smiled. "Char—I'm sure you'll figure out a way to work with him. After all, you don't have much of a choice."

"Not true." Charlotte shook her head. "There has to be some way to get rid of him." With Gretchen as a real estate professional, she hoped she'd have an idea about how to make Luke move his truck to another space.

"I don't see how," Maggie said. "There isn't much vacant land in town and that's a prime spot."

"He's got a lease, right?" Gretchen asked. "You didn't rent the whole space from Mr. Devine and he leased the other half." She shrugged. "I think you're stuck with him. That is, unless you want to move somewhere else. Isn't your lease up soon?"

Charlotte stared at her in horror. "No! I was there first. Whimsical Delights is in the perfect place to get tourist traffic. He can move." Her lease was up soon, but she had every intention of renewing it. Luke Tisdale wasn't going to make her move.

"I would think that's why he wants to have his truck there too," Maggie said carefully.

Charlotte didn't respond, instead choosing to open her menu. Inside though, she was fuming. She'd expected her friends to back her up on this, but they seemed to be taking Luke's side.

Reading through the familiar menu, she felt a little calmer. While she read, her friends chatted with each other to give her space. Smooth jazz drifted across the room, helping her to relax.

She folded up the menu and set it down on the table before drinking some of her ice water. The chilly drink reminded her of Luke's attempt to apologize that had turned into soaking her with water. She set the glass on the table and pushed it toward the wall, far away from her.

"How was the art show last week?" Gretchen asked. "I don't think I've seen you since then."

Charlotte felt a smile creep across her face. Although Gretchen liked to tease her, she always seemed to know how to make her feel better. "It was amazing. They loved my paintings, especially the one of the sun setting over the ocean." The elation of having her artistic talents recognized at the gallery show rushed over her.

"Ooh, I love that one too," Maggie said. "I'm happy they liked it.

Charlotte took a deep breath. "In fact, the gallery owner mentioned the possibility of me having my own show."

"Really?" Gretchen set down her wine glass. "When?"

"He didn't say, but I think sometime fairly soon." Her smile slipped. If she wanted a successful show, she needed to start burning the midnight oil to have something to sell.

Since she'd returned from her trip to Seattle, it seemed like everything she'd started was garbage. That was another negative point about Luke and his food truck. She'd been so caught up in being mad at him that her muse had flown the coop.

"Well, let us know when it is. We'll all be there." Maggie picked up the menu. "Now, does anyone want to order more food?"

"Me!" Gretchen said. "Let's try something off the new menu items." She gestured to a small sheet of paper attached to the front of the formal menu that Charlotte hadn't noticed. "I think we should get that dessert to share too. I can smell the chocolate from here." She pointed at a luscious dark chocolate torte that the couple at the next table over were digging into.

Charlotte reached for her menu and checked the new items. Although it was a minor thing, with all the changes in her life at the moment, something as simple as a menu change made her heart sink. Nothing ever stayed the same.

6
———

*B*laring sirens from the town's fire trucks woke Charlotte at three o'clock on Tuesday morning. She sat up in bed with a start and threw on her bathrobe, icy fear rendering her fully awake. The bookstore wasn't connected to the neighboring buildings, and they'd added an automatic fire sprinkler system after a madman had set it on fire two years ago, but she still didn't want to be caught unaware if the fire ripped through downtown.

She padded to the open window in her socks and looked out. Everything around the bookstore appeared to be fine, but she could still hear the sirens not too far down the street. She hurriedly slipped on a T-shirt and jeans and clopped down the interior stairs wearing sandals over her socks.

Although it was the end of May, chilly night air blasted her when she stepped outside. She grabbed Dahlia's sweater from a hook by the back door and wrapped it around her body before walking down the street. She walked two blocks down Main Street and stopped at the next corner. Just down the street, the Bike Barn's roof was afire, flames shooting skyward.

The firemen seemed to have it under control, so her apartment and To Be Read didn't appear to be in any danger, but she stayed to watch. Saul, the owner of the Bike Barn, stood off to the side watching his business go up in smoke. Near him, several other people had gathered.

Her stomach twisted. As a business owner herself, she had an inkling of how this would impact him. The tourist season was in full swing and even if he could rebuild the store and order more inventory, he'd lose out on a few months of revenue at the very least.

She moved closer to the fire trucks.

"I'm sorry, miss. I need you to stay back," a fireman said to her.

She nodded. The air was heavy with acrid smoke and the odor of burning rubber from all of the bike tires Saul had kept in the store.

"How horrible for Saul," a familiar voice said from behind her.

Charlotte turned to find Maggie standing there, shivering, with her bare arms wrapped across her chest.

She gave Maggie a quizzical look.

"Jake is on the night shift," she said, referring to her fiancé, a police officer in Candle Beach. "He called to let me know about the fire, in case the Bluebonnet Café was in danger." She cast a glance at her restaurant a block up from the fire.

"Ah."

They both stared at the fire again. Orange flames licked at what remained of the wood structure.

"That place is Saul's life," Maggie said. "He moved here

to start fresh after his wife died and he told me he used all of his savings to buy it. I feel horrible for him."

"Do you think it's a complete loss?"

"Oh yeah, look at that." Maggie pointed at a beam leaning to the side. "His stock room was at the back, and it's totally gone."

The firemen were still spraying water at the building. She and Maggie were so close to the fire hydrant that they could hear the water rushing through the hoses before it shot out the nozzles and rained to the ground.

"At least it's not too windy tonight," Charlotte said, mesmerized by the fire. Although it seemed wrong to think it, she wondered if she could reproduce the colors of the flames on a canvas.

"I think they've got it," Maggie said. "I'd better get back home. I woke up Alex and threw him in the car when Jake called, but he's got school tomorrow."

Charlotte nodded. "I should get back too." She checked her watch. "I have to open the shop in five hours."

She walked with Maggie back to her car. Her six-year-old son Alex had fallen asleep in his booster seat, his head resting against the window.

Maggie sighed. "That kid can fall asleep anywhere. I hope I can get him awake enough to move him into the apartment. He's getting too big to carry."

"Good luck," Charlotte said.

"I'll need it." Maggie stared at Alex and shook her head. "Good night." She got into her car and drove away.

Charlotte continued walking back up the hill to the bookstore. By this time, she was wide awake, but still exhausted at the same time. She climbed back into bed and stared at the ceiling. Her fight with Luke seemed petty in light of what Saul must be going through. If Whimsical

Delights caught on fire or she lost her paintings to some sort of disaster, she'd be devastated.

Was she wrong to be mad at Luke? The memory of him calling her Chatty Charlie whispered in her brain. At this point, she wasn't ready to forgive him, but for the sake of their businesses and for Parker, she'd make an effort to be civil to him.

Luke shifted in his seat in the town hall as he waited for the meeting to begin. Candle Beach's mayor, Chester Raines, had called a town meeting to address the fire at the Bike Barn. The room buzzed as everyone got settled into the collapsible metal chairs that had been crammed into the main hall, which hadn't been built for such a large attendance.

"I'm sure all of you have heard about what happened to the Bike Barn," Mayor Raines said as he looked out over the packed main room.

The crowd murmured.

"Do they know how long it'll take to rebuild?" a man asked.

Mayor Raines shook his head. "I don't think so. Probably not before summer ends."

"I can't believe this happened, so soon after the bookstore's fire," a woman sitting in the chair next to him said to her friend on the other side of her.

"Is there anything we can do to help?" a woman asked from the front of the room. She was hidden from his view by two taller men wearing ball caps, but he recognized Charlotte's voice.

He straightened. He'd gotten off on the wrong foot with

her and he wasn't sure how to rectify the situation. Although she'd been annoying as his best friend's kid sister, over the years she'd blossomed into a beautiful woman who seemed to be a kind and generous person.

She may consider him the enemy now, but he hoped to one day have a good working relationship with her. They'd need it if they expected both of their businesses to succeed on the small lot they shared. If only he hadn't called her Chatty Charlie. The nickname had just popped out of him when he'd been surprised to see her, but he couldn't change that now.

The mayor cleared his throat before responding. "That's actually the reason I called this meeting. I'd like to see the town help Saul. Maybe someone has a rental space for him to operate out of while his store is being rebuilt? Then he won't lose so much money this summer."

"I have a small garage space I'm not using near the grocery store. He could use that," an elderly man volunteered.

Mayor Raines beamed. "Excellent. That's the kind of solution I'm looking for."

"How about a fundraiser? He's always helped out everyone in town, so I bet a lot of people would want to donate to the cause," Charlotte said.

"I can volunteer the Sorensen Farm barn," a woman said. "With my upcoming wedding, I can't take on the project of organizing it, but you're welcome to have some sort of fundraiser at the barn. Jake and I would love to help out Saul."

Next to her, a man nodded. "We can provide all of the catering supplies and the venue, but we'll need someone to bring the food and other things, depending on what type of event it is."

"Thank you, Maggie and Jake. That's generous of you," Mayor Raines said. "Is there anyone who can take on the task of organizing an event?"

There were rumblings in the crowd, and chairs squeaked as everyone looked around to see if anyone would volunteer, but no one stepped up.

Ever since he'd arrived in Candle Beach, Luke had felt like an outsider. Maybe this was his chance to become part of the fabric of the town.

"I'll help," he said, standing.

At the same time Charlotte stood and said, "I can do it."

She turned at the sound of his voice and their eyes met. He could feel her eyes shooting daggers at him from across the room.

"I said I can organize it," she said stubbornly.

Mayor Raines laughed nervously. "Well, two volunteers. That's great." He turned to Luke. "I'm sorry, I don't think I caught your name."

"I'm Luke Tisdale. I just moved to town and I own the Beachside BBQ food truck." He scanned the crowd as he spoke. People were nodding and murmuring to each other.

"Ah. Of course. I've seen your truck. I'm looking forward to trying your barbecue sometime this week. You know, this sounds like a big job. It will be great if the two of you can work together to make the fundraiser a success," the mayor said. He turned his attention to the others. "Does anyone else have any suggestions?"

"Just don't make the fundraiser a bake sale," a woman with a tight bun said. "I hate bake sales and they never make much money."

Mayor Raines smiled. "I think what Agnes is saying is that it needs to be something bigger so that we can really help Saul out. I'm sure Charlotte and Luke will figure something out, but if they need help, we're all there for them." He addressed the crowd. "Thank you all for coming. That's what I love about this town—everyone comes together to help a fellow citizen in need." A wide smile stretched across his face.

Everyone stood and started to file out of the room. Before Charlotte could exit, Luke caught her arm and pulled her aside. She froze when he touched her arm, but she turned to talk to him.

"Yes?"

"Look, I didn't mean to step on your toes, but I'd like to help. I can provide barbecue for the event." He smiled, hoping to disarm her.

She took a deep breath. "I don't need your help, but it looks like we're stuck together anyway. I don't have time tonight, but I can meet tomorrow evening to discuss the fundraiser if you'd like."

So, the ice princess was thawing a little. He'd wondered if she'd ever talk to him. It had taken a fire for her to finally do so. For the sake of his friendship with Parker, he'd like for them to be cordial to each other, but if she refused to talk to him, that wouldn't happen.

"That would be great." He flashed her a smile, determined to kill her with kindness. "How about seven o'clock? We can meet at the café or something."

"Yeah, fine. That works." She edged backward as though she couldn't wait to get away from him. "I've got to get going, but I'll see you tomorrow." She rushed out of the room.

Behind him, some men were stacking the metal chairs against the wall, and he went over to help. The monotonous work of picking up one chair after another cleared his mind a little, allowing him to think. Why was he letting Charlotte get to him so much? He'd encountered people before that he didn't get along with, but this was different. Something about her was different, but he couldn't quite put his finger on it.

Their first meeting regarding the Bike Barn fundraiser had been short and to the point. They'd settled on a date for the fundraiser for the middle of July and Luke had confirmed that he'd be providing barbecue for the event. Charlotte had said she'd take care of everything else. When he'd protested, she'd told him they could talk about it at their next meeting.

Now that the second meeting had arrived, Luke wasn't sure what he wanted the outcome to be. She'd made it pretty clear that she wanted as little to do with him as possible. Did he want to force his help on her? He glanced out the big front window of the food truck over to her Airstream. She'd put off the second meeting several times, claiming to be too busy to meet. This was a big project for one person to take on by themselves, and he had a feeling that she was too stubborn to ask for help.

Yeah, he was going to make her accept his help. He went outside and shut the wooden flap over the front window and cleared the condiments from the metal bar on the outside of the trailer. Chances were Charlotte hadn't had dinner yet, and since they were meeting at one of his picnic tables as soon as she closed her shop, he'd bring her something. Food always helped to mend things between people.

He fixed a heaping platter of barbecued brisket and smoked macaroni and cheese, then peeked out the back door. She'd picked up the items outside of her trailer as she did every night before closing and taken down the sandwich board she always set on the sidewalk to lure customers in. It was showtime.

He placed the food, paper plates and plastic forks down

on a picnic table and knocked on the closed trailer door. She opened it a crack.

"Yes?"

"We're supposed to meet tonight about the fundraiser, remember?" He felt surprisingly unsure of himself. Something about Charlotte threw him off guard.

A pained expression crossed her face and she opened the door wider. "Oh yeah." She glanced at a calendar on the wall behind her. "Give me a minute and I'll meet you outside."

He nodded and sat down at the picnic table. Should he dish out some food? Or leave it for her to serve herself?

"What's all this?" She came out of the trailer and pointed at the food.

"I thought you might like some dinner." He gave her what he hoped was a disarming smile.

"Uh." She eyed the food hungrily as she set her white binder down on the table. "Sure, I guess I could try some."

He felt as if he'd scored a goal. "Here." He scooped out some mac 'n' cheese and plopped it on her plate, followed by the smoked barbecue brisket.

She picked up her fork and he held his breath, waiting for the verdict. He'd topped the brisket with some pickled red onions and a swirl of his signature sweet and spicy barbecue sauce.

The brisket went into her mouth and her eyes closed for a moment, as if she was savoring the taste. She swallowed, then set her fork down and pushed the plate to the side. "It's spicy."

"Oh." He wasn't sure he'd hidden his disappointment very well. "I could get you a new plate of brisket with the sweet sauce on it."

"Don't bother. I'm not that hungry." She opened up her

notebook and his eyes widened. Neat, multi-colored tabs bore labels for each main item of the fundraiser – the silent auction, food, marketing, tickets, and more. Maybe she *was* Super Woman and could handle this on her own.

"You've got the food and Maggie's offered up the Sorensen Farm for the venue, so we're set on that." She tapped the end of her pen against her lips. "I'll take care of advertising and decorations. I guess you could help with procuring items for the silent auction."

He was still in awe of her organization and found it difficult to speak. "Uh, sure. I can do that."

"There's been some money donated from local businesses to get the fundraiser off the ground, but it's not a lot, so we'll have to keep that in mind." She showed him the figures she'd written out for the budget. While he was reviewing it, he caught her gaze slide over to the brisket and he could have sworn she licked her lips, but he didn't comment on it.

He nodded. "Looks good."

"Great." She gave him a tight-lipped smile and flipped the front cover of her binder closed. "We can meet again sometime next week to check in." She stood from the table and went back into her trailer, shutting the door firmly behind her.

He sat at the table for a moment, then grabbed the uneaten food and dug in. The peace offering had been a miserable failure. He wasn't expecting them to ever be best friends, but he'd hoped that this meeting would have made things a little warmer between the two of them. That idea had flopped as badly as the smoked brisket.

A week later, Charlotte was sitting on her living room couch working on the plans for the Bike Barn fundraiser when her phone rang. She eyed the phone, which was charging on the kitchen counter and then the lapful of binder inserts she was working on. *I'd probably better get that.* She eased the notebook pages off of her lap and onto the couch cushion, then made a mad dash for the kitchen, reaching the phone just in time before it went to voicemail.

"Hello?" She tried to calm her breathing.

"Hello. This is Raymond Donohue, calling from the Donohue Gallery. Is this Charlotte?"

"It is. Hi, Raymond."

"I wanted to follow up with you on scheduling a show of your work next month. Are you still interested in the opportunity?"

Was she still interested? Ha! She was having trouble keeping herself from squealing for joy at the moment.

"Yes. I'd love to show my paintings at the gallery."

"Fantastic. I have it scheduled for Thursday, July fifth. You can drop off your artwork either Monday or Tuesday of that week."

"Thank you so much for this opportunity. I appreciate it."

"Well, I'm sure our patrons will love your artwork just as much as I did," he said warmly. "I have to get going now, but I'll see you in a month, all right?"

"Yes. Thank you," she said. "See you in a month."

He hung up and she allowed herself to do a victory dance on the linoleum kitchen floors. "Woohoo!" She screamed out loud.

"Are you okay up there?" Dahlia shouted from the bottom of the stairs.

Charlotte laughed as she opened the door. "I'm fine.

More than fine. The art gallery just called to schedule my solo show."

Dahlia walked up the stairs to Charlotte's apartment. "That's great. When is it?"

"July fifth ." Charlotte couldn't stop beaming.

Dahlia's face fell. "Oh. Sad. Garrett and I will be gone on our trip to Europe."

Charlotte hugged her. "Don't worry about it. I would have loved for you to come to my showing, but you're going to have so much fun seeing the art of the old masters in Italy. I'm jealous."

Dahlia glanced at the easel Charlotte had set up in her living room. "July fifth isn't too far away. Do you know yet which pieces you'll have in the show?"

Charlotte followed her friend's gaze and her good mood slumped slightly. A month wasn't too far away and there was still so much she wanted to get done for the show.

"I'm not sure yet." Charlotte bit her lip. "It's going to be like picking which of my babies I love the best."

Dahlia smiled. "I'm sure they'll love anything you have."

"I hope so." Charlotte smiled. "I think this calls for a celebration." She walked into the kitchen and selected a bottle of champagne from the refrigerator. "I've been saving this one for a special occasion and I think this qualifies. Want to share with me?"

"I wouldn't miss out on this celebration." Dahlia squeezed her with one arm. "I'm so excited for you."

Charlotte glowed inside. This was her chance to show all of her friends and family that she could succeed in the art world. Her parents had been telling her for years that she'd never be a commercial success and she hoped to prove them wrong with this show. She grabbed two champagne glasses from the cupboard and set them on the table, then uncorked the bottle. When the fizziness had subsided, she poured it into the two glasses and they held them up in the air.

"To the best painter I know," Dahlia clinked her glass against Charlotte's and they sipped their drinks. Bubbles went up her nose, adding to the giddy sensations she was feeling. She had a lot of work in front of her to get ready for the show, but for now, she was going to celebrate.

7
———

*I*t never failed to amaze Luke how barbecue sauce could get into every nook and cranny in the food truck. That didn't matter though—every mess he cleaned up reminded him that he had customers and people liked his food. He swiped at a glob of light-brown sweet sauce that had hardened on the counter, releasing a faint scent of honey and spice into the air. Locals and tourists alike had gone nuts over the three sauces he'd carefully concocted for the food truck and the tender, fall-off-the-bone meats he smoked out back.

Although it hadn't been the reason he'd volunteered to cater the fundraiser for the Bike Barn, it should bring him new business too. It never hurt to get the name of his business in front of potential customers. That is, if he and Charlotte could manage to work together and pull the fundraiser off without making both of them look like fools.

Luke had no doubt that Charlotte had everything under control with the fundraiser, but although they worked only ten feet from each other, she was hard to pin down for a time to meet. He'd had a few questions about the auction

47

items and had resorted to sticking a note on her trailer door with his question on it. He'd found a response taped to his food truck's door the next morning. Judging by her lack of availability, she probably had a boyfriend or something that she spent all of her time with, but she certainly hadn't told him that.

A strong emotion shot through his chest when he thought about Charlotte, surprising him. Was he jealous of the boyfriend or upset because she didn't have enough time to commit to the event?

He finished polishing the counter to a high shine that would make a food inspector sing with delight, then threw the rag into a bucket near the door to take home to wash. He'd found a small studio apartment nearby to rent for the time being. It was only a tenth of the size of the condo he'd owned in the Bay Area, but somehow, it suited him.

Everything looked good inside, so he grabbed the bucket and locked up, pausing on the steps to survey the lot with a critical eye. The six stools for the long eating bar he'd set up against the back of the lot were tucked under it and the wooden picnic tables and round table with chairs had been hosed off for the day. All was good out here too.

He'd done a particularly thorough clean that day and the sun was already starting to set. He stretched, then sat down at a picnic table with his back against the tabletop to relax and watch nature's majestic show, something he'd always enjoyed growing up.

Pinks and oranges streaked the sky as the sun fell slowly downward into the ocean. From this elevation, he couldn't see past the trees lining the tall cliffs that flanked the sandy beaches, but the roar of the Pacific Ocean carried well into town. The tree branches provided an interesting frame for the sunset and he found his gaze pulled to it.

He put his feet up on one of the wood chairs from nearby and leaned back against the picnic table, closing his eyes. The air still held a touch of warmth, and although he was exhausted from a long day, the peacefulness of the scene kept him there instead of heading home.

"Oh, drat," a woman's voice said as something clattered onto the gravel in between his truck and Charlotte's trailer.

His eyes popped open and he looked around. No one else was in the lot with him, so where had that come from? He looked up.

In the dimming light, he saw Charlotte perched on the roof of the Airstream, a small easel and canvas set up in front of her. She was intent on her painting and didn't seem to notice him. He sat there, watching her.

She was silhouetted against the sky and from what he could see from this angle, had been painting the sunset he'd been admiring. Her blonde hair fluttered around her shoulders in the breeze. From here, she looked like a captivating fairy—a very beautiful one. His breath caught.

What was he thinking? This was his friend's sister, not some woman he'd met in a bar. Even if there was any chance she'd ever be attracted to him, she was off-limits.

He walked over to where he'd heard something drop to the gravel. A piece of artists' charcoal lay on the ground, unbroken. He plucked it from between two small rocks and held it up to her.

"Do you need this?"

She leaned over the top of the trailer and stared at him in surprise.

"I didn't know anyone was here." She stretched her arm out for the charcoal and he passed it up to her. "Thank you."

"I didn't know anyone was here either. It was so quiet." He stood there awkwardly for a moment, hoping that she'd offer him a nugget of conversation to indicate she might be ready for a truce. "It's a nice night."

"It is." She eyed him and looked like she was about to say something, then sat upright and pointed at the canvas in front of her. "If you don't mind, I'd like to finish this."

He raised his eyebrows. "Of course. I'll leave you be."

Without another word, she moved her attention back to her work.

He grabbed the bucket with the soiled rags and walked the seven blocks to his apartment. What was going on with Charlotte? It seemed like she'd been about to say something nice and have a normal conversation with him, but then had reverted back to her old standoffish self. He didn't know if he was making any progress with her or if she had no intention of ever forgiving him for his blunders the first day they'd seen each other on the shared lot.

When he reached his apartment, he opened the door and brought the rags into the laundry area in the bathroom to wash. Afterward, he found himself pacing the small studio. Although it was usually plenty of room for him, today he felt as though he was trapped in there. Quickly, he changed his clothes, threw on his sneakers and jogged off toward the beach. Maybe he could run off all the conflicting emotions about Charlotte that were swirling through his head. Or, he could further exhaust himself enough that he'd fall asleep easily without having to think of her again until the next day.

8
------

*L*uke entered Pete's Pizzeria at half past six and scanned the pizza joint for Parker. He'd been in town for four weeks already, but he and his best friend had both been so busy that this was the first time they'd been able to clear time in their schedules for dinner together. On a Thursday night, the restaurant was busy, but not crowded, and he spotted Parker right away, sitting in a booth near the corner.

"Is the food any good here?" Luke asked as he slid into the bench seat across from his friend.

Parker grinned. "It's the best pizza in Candle Beach."

Luke raised an eyebrow. "That's not saying much."

Parker laughed at his joke. "No, seriously, Pete's rivals any place in the city."

Luke had his doubts about that. In San Francisco, he'd had a favorite place to get pizza and no one could do a deep-dish pizza like Tony's. "We'll see."

"Do you still like sausage and mushroom?" Parker asked.

Luke nodded. When they'd been starving teenage boys, between the two of them, they'd easily consumed a large sausage and mushroom pizza during an afternoon study session. While he didn't think he could handle that much pizza now, it was still his favorite combination.

The waitress came around and they placed their pizza order and requested two beers. Luke wanted to ask Parker about Charlotte, but as soon as they'd ordered, his friend launched into a lengthy description of his new real estate company. Much as he wanted to pay attention, he found his mind wandering. Why did Charlotte hate him so much?

They'd been there for twenty minutes before he was able to cut in and broach the subject of Charlotte.

"So, what's the deal with your sister?" Luke asked.

"Which one?"

"Charlotte. The one that's here in town." He'd almost forgotten that Parker had another brother and sister. The concept of having so much family was alien to him, as it had just been himself, his sister and their grandparents for as long as he could remember growing up.

"What do you mean?" Parker asked carefully.

"Does she hate me, or what?" He picked up his frosty beer mug and took a big gulp from it.

Parker shrugged. "I don't know. I haven't talked with her much lately. She's been so busy with the shop and preparing for an art show. She doesn't have much time for anything else." He looked at Luke more closely. "Why do you ask? Is she still mad about you moving into that space next to her?"

"Yes. I don't think she's ever going to get over it."

Parker smiled. "Charlotte can hold a grudge, that's for sure. One time when we were kids, I used one of her Barbie dolls for an outdoor camping adventure with my GI Joes, and let's just say Barbie didn't return looking the same. I thought she'd never forgive me. But even for her, that's a little ridiculous. It's not like you did anything wrong."

The waitress brought over their sausage and mushroom deep-dish pizza and placed the steaming pie on a pedestal in the middle of their table.

Luke took a slice and bit into it, gooey cheese dripping everywhere. His eyes widened and he went in for another bite. "I thought I was going to miss my favorite pizza place in San Francisco, but this is even better." It didn't even matter that he burned his tongue with every bite he took. It was that amazing.

"How's it going here? Has business been good? I always see a line in front of the food truck at lunchtime." Parker took a bite too, then set his pizza down on his plate to wash it down with a swig of beer. "Man, that's hot. You must have a Teflon tongue to not feel that."

He smiled. "No, but I'm hungry. I've been smelling barbecue all day and dreaming of pizza."

Parker laughed.

"I like it here," Luke said. "It's nice to be back near Pops." After he'd moved to California, he hadn't seen his grandparents nearly as much as he'd wanted to, or should have done. When his grandmother died, he'd only been able to take a few days away from work to attend her funeral and help his grandfather get things settled. He took another bite of pizza and swallowed before continuing. "I'd be a lot happier if your sister wasn't glaring at me from the steps of her shop all day."

"It can't be that bad, right?" Parker narrowed his eyes at Luke. "Why's she so mad at you? It's not just the sharing a lot thing, is it?"

Luke wiped his hands on the paper napkin and twisted it between his fingers. "I may have called her Chatty Charlie when we first met."

"She's mad about that? I mean, I know she hated it when

we called her that back in high school, but it doesn't seem like that big of a deal."

"That's all I can think of, other than she's not happy having me anywhere near her shop."

"I'll ask her about it. Other than that, how are things? I heard you and Charlotte are working together on a benefit event for the Bike Barn."

He nodded. "We are. Which is another reason why I'd love it if she'd talk to me. Do you know how difficult it is to get things done when your co-planner won't talk to you?"

Parker raised an eyebrow and then grabbed another slice of pizza. "I can imagine. I'll talk to her. Maybe I can arrange a peace treaty or something." He looked at Luke. "You seem awfully concerned with what Charlotte thinks of you. Do you have a thing for her or something?"

Luke pushed himself as far back on the booth seat as he could and raised his hands defensively. "No, no. Of course not. Besides, she has a boyfriend." He flagged the waitress over and asked for a refill on his beer.

"Uh, as far as I know, there's no boyfriend in the picture." Parker laughed. "She doesn't have time for anything except the shop and her art. Mom's been complaining that she hasn't heard from her in a month."

Luke took in that piece of information. He'd assumed that Charlotte had a boyfriend that was taking up all her free time, but this put a different spin on things. He tried to push that thought away.

"She's your sister."

"Yeah, she's my sister, not yours."

"Well, in my mind, she's off-limits, even if she'd give me the time of day. But she won't, so it's not an issue." He turned the tables on Parker. "How are you and Gretchen? Is it weird working together?"

Parker and Gretchen had started a new real estate company together in the area and had recently become engaged. He couldn't imagine working with someone he was that close to, but then again, he'd never had a relationship get to that point either, so what did he know?

Parker lit up. "It's great. We have our differences sometimes, but you know how it is—when you work long hours, it's hard to see your loved ones. This way I get to see Gretchen every day."

Luke watched his friend's face as he spoke of his fiancée. Before meeting Gretchen, Parker had been somewhat of a playboy, so it was a bit of a shock to see him so devoted. A familiar sense of jealousy shot through him, just as it had when he was thinking about Charlotte's boyfriend.

Why was he thinking like that though? With a new business, he didn't have time for dating, much less dating Charlotte.

When Charlotte came home from the shop on Friday night, the bookstore was closed for business, but was full of people. Garrett and Dahlia were leaving for their European vacation the next day and would be gone for over a month.

Charlotte went upstairs first to put her stuff away and then came back down to join the party. Her apartment was empty, but the voices from below filled the space. Her comfy couch and TV were calling her name and part of her didn't want to go downstairs. Before she could get too fond of the idea of staying in for the night, she forced herself to go down the stairs.

The guests of honor were holding court under a *Bon Voyage* streamer near the espresso bar, which had been turned into a hosted bar for the evening. Dahlia threw back her head and laughed at something Garrett's mother Meg said, her face flushed with happiness. Garrett wrapped his arm around her waist and pulled her close.

Gretchen and Parker were chatting with Maggie and Jake in the corner. Charlotte's heart ached at the sight of all the happy couples. She just needed to keep telling herself that she had her art and the shop. There wasn't time for anything else. Her stomach grumbled and the table in the corner piled high with food called her name. She made way over there to check out the selection. It looked like the Blue-bonnet Café had catered the party, but was that a serving dish full of Luke's barbecue in the back? She looked around but didn't see him and figured it was safe to take some.

A scoop of shredded barbecued chicken went on her plate, along with the sweet and spicy barbecue sauce he'd given her to try the week before. She dipped her fork in it and took a bite before leaving the table. It was just as amazing as it had been before—although there was no way she'd ever let Luke know that.

Someone poked her shoulder and she almost jumped, hastily wiping away any sign of barbecue sauce from her lips before turning around. Luckily, it was only Parker.

"Hey," she said with relief.

"Hey. I've been meaning to talk to you."

She tilted her head up. "What about? Is everything okay?"

"Everything's fine, don't worry. I had dinner with Luke last night and he said the two of you were working on the Bike Barn fundraiser together." He peered at her. "How's that going?"

"Oh, fine. I could have managed well enough on my own

though." She frowned. If Luke hadn't volunteered, things would have been much easier.

Parker's eyes danced with mirth. "I'm sure you could have. But it's nice for him to get involved. He's new in town, remember?"

"Yeah? So?" She winced at the harshness in her tone, but she couldn't take it back.

"So, you could give him a break." Parker's eyes drilled into her face.

"Did he say something to you?" That took some nerve, complaining about her to her brother.

"He mentioned that you didn't seem too happy to have him helping."

"Well, he's right. I'm not." She eyed the barbecue on her plate. Her mouth was salivating for another bite, but she didn't want to eat it in front of Parker.

"Charlotte. Give him a chance, okay? You don't have to be best friends, but I'd like for the two of you to get along. If he did something to offend you, I'm sure it wasn't on purpose."

Her resolve softened and she rolled her eyes. "Okay. I'll be nicer about his helping. Happy?"

"Yes." He grinned at her and slugged her on the shoulder. "See ya later, sis."

She watched him walk away, then took another bite of barbecue. The chicken was so tender that it melted in her mouth, blending with the sweetness and spice of the sauce.

"Do you like it?" A voice said from behind her.

She whirled around. Luke. She quickly placed her napkin over the plate. "I'm sorry?"

"The barbecue." He pointed at her plate and the concealed chicken. "Did you like it?" His voice held a hint of uncertainty, probably because she'd spat it out last time she'd tasted it in front of him.

"I don't know what you're talking about." She walked over to a garbage can and threw the plate in. It hurt to throw such delicious food away, but she didn't have any other choice.

"Oh. I thought you had some."

She felt his eyes on her face and she suddenly felt self-conscious. "What?"

"You've got something right there." He reached out and brushed her cheek with his thumb.

Her breath caught at the sensations that rippled through her body from his delicate touch, followed quickly by indignation. "Do you mind?"

He examined a splotch of red on his thumb. "Looks a lot like barbecue sauce." His lips quivered, as though he were fighting to hide a smile.

She opened and closed her mouth like a guppy. *Argh! He made her so mad. There was definitely no way she could admit to him now that she'd loved the barbecue.* She stared at him without saying a word, then walked away.

When she'd distanced herself from him, she silently scolded herself. Why had she lied to him? She'd just told her brother she'd try to be nice to him, but there was something about Luke Tisdale that got her all riled up. She looked around for someone to talk to, her eyes landing on a woman sitting alone in the corner, looking as lonely as she felt.

"Hey," Charlotte said. "Sarah, right?"

The woman nodded and tucked her brunette hair behind her ears. "Yes. And you're Charlotte, Parker's sister, right?"

Charlotte smiled. "I am." She pulled up a chair next to Sarah. "How's it going?"

"Great. I'm a teacher, and school is almost over for the summer, so I'm happy about that." She looked at Charlotte. "Did Dahlia tell you I'm managing the bookstore for her while she's gone?"

"She said something about someone taking over for her, but she didn't say who. I'm the one who lives in the apartment above the store, so we'll see a lot of each other over the next few months." Charlotte looked around the room. "Not to be nosy, but are you dating anyone?"

Sarah laughed. "Nope, I'm going to be an old maid." She made a face. "Why, do you have someone to fix me up with?"

"No, but I'm starting to feel like the proverbial third wheel at this party. Everyone here seems to have brought a date." She motioned to all the couples in the room. "It's refreshing to meet someone else in the same boat as me."

"We'll have to start an old maid's club," Sarah quipped. "Then again, I thought my brother Adam would be a bachelor forever and he's dating someone now. Maybe there's hope for us yet."

"Maybe." Charlotte stared wistfully at Parker, who was now standing with his arm around Gretchen. She wouldn't have thought her brother would ever settle down, but he'd met Gretchen and that had been the end of his single life. It seemed like fate with them, as they'd met when Charlotte rented Gretchen's house when she first moved to town. Well, they'd officially met before that, but she liked to think she'd brought them together.

All her friends had found their matches and she was running out of eligible bachelors in town. It would have to be a newcomer to Candle Beach. An image of Luke popped into her head. He may not be high on her list of potential mates, but he was an eligible bachelor. As if on cue, he crossed her line of sight. She eyed him as he walked over to Parker and Gretchen to join their conversation. She had promised Parker to be nice to him. Maybe some match-making was in order.

"I might know someone to fix you up with," she said.

"Really?" Sarah perked up.

"Yeah. A friend of my brother's. He's not too bad-looking and he's really smart." She felt a small twinge describing Luke's attractive qualities.

"Does he have a job?" Sarah asked. "It seems like everyone I've met recently is unemployed and not really looking."

"Kind of?" Charlotte smiled. "He owns a food truck."

"Hmm." Sarah appeared to consider it. "I'd love to meet someone with ambition, although at this point, I'll take any adult male that can carry on a conversation. I've spent all year with fourth-graders. I need to spend some time with adults. I mean really, look at me here. I've spilled my life story to you and we hardly know each other."

Charlotte laughed. "Don't worry about it. Sometimes I feel the same way. All I ever do is paint and work. I don't think I even have time for someone to sweep me off my feet."

Sarah laughed. "Not even Prince Charming?"

"If Prince Charming came to Candle Beach, I'd go out with him. Anyone else I don't have time for." She checked her watch and glanced over at Luke, who was still chatting with someone. She'd have to introduce him to Sarah later. "Speaking of Prince Charming and fairy tales, I'm going to turn into a pumpkin soon if I don't get to bed." She stood from the chair. "It was nice talking with you. I'm sure we'll see each other a lot this summer with Dahlia gone. And if you ever start up an old maid's club, make sure you tell me. I'd love to join."

"I will." Sarah smiled at her. "It was nice talking with you too."

Charlotte approached Dahlia and Garrett to wish them a safe journey.

"Hey," she said, tapping Dahlia on the shoulder.

"Char! I'm so glad to see you here." Dahlia laughed. "This party has been so much fun. I'm thinking Garrett and I should entertain more. Did you get something to eat or drink?"

"I did." Guilty memories of the delicious barbecue ran through her mind. If Luke hadn't still been present, she would have gone back for more.

"I heard you and Luke were working together on the fundraiser for the Bike Barn. Maybe things will heat up between the two of you. He's quite a catch." Dahlia winked at her.

When had Dahlia met Luke? Oh right, when she let him into Charlotte's apartment.

"We're not exactly friends."

"Oh?" Dahlia cocked her head to the side. "I'm sorry. I thought you were. He said you'd known each other since childhood."

"Yes. We have. But calling us friends is stretching it quite a bit."

"I wouldn't have let him in if I'd known." Dahlia's eyes became troubled and Charlotte felt horrible. She hadn't meant to bring her friend down when she should be enjoying her party.

"Don't worry about it." Charlotte flashed her a smile.

"It's not like he was there to kill me or something." She laughed to let Dahlia know everything was okay.

"Well, I'm glad you two are working together on the fundraiser. Maybe you can mend whatever relationship you have." She frowned. "But I'm bummed I'll miss the event. We're coming back the day before Maggie's wedding, but we won't be back in time for the Bike Barn fundraiser."

"That's okay," Charlotte said. "You know, there's still time to donate an auction item to make up for it." A gleam formed in her eyes.

Dahlia laughed. "Okay, okay, I can take a hint. I'll drop something off at your apartment before we leave tomorrow."

"Thanks!" Charlotte cast a glance toward the back of the bookstore. "I'm exhausted though. I think I'm heading up for the night."

"Oh, sad," Dahlia said. "The party's just beginning."

"Yeah, but I've got too much to do. I think I'm going to work on my painting and then hit the hay." She gave Dahlia a hug. "I'll miss you though."

Her friend hugged her back. "I'll miss you too. Did you meet Sarah?"

Charlotte nodded. "I did. She seems nice. She's Adam's sister, right?"

"Yes. I think she'll do a good job with the bookstore while I'm gone. She already has some great ideas for the children's section."

"I bet that with being a teacher, she'll be a huge asset in that area." She glanced back at Sarah, who was standing in a corner talking to Maggie, and then looked at the door to the back room. "Well, I'd better get going. Have a safe trip." Charlotte hugged her again and left, trudging up the stairs to her apartment.

To drown out the party noise coming through the floorboards, she stuffed wireless earbuds into her ears and turned up the volume on her phone to stream the classical music station she favored. It always helped her get in the right mood for painting. A few days ago, she'd started a landscape of Bluebonnet Lake, but something wasn't quite right about it—the lake wasn't the correct shade of blue. As much as she loved to paint, it frustrated her when she wasn't able to capture what she could see in her mind's eye. She fussed with the color until she was satisfied with it. An hour later, she hadn't quite finished, but she was too tired to put in any more effort without making major mistakes.

On a whim, she pulled out her sketchpad and sat down on the couch. She'd been to Europe with her parents as a teenager, but she had never been as an adult. How amazing would it be to go to Paris and sketch? Or to have someone special to experience it all with her? Her pencil moved across the paper. When she was done, she stared at it. For some reason, she'd drawn Luke, looking out over a river. Why? She stared at it until her eyes glazed over and she ripped it out and balled it up. This was ridiculous. She was so tired that she was drawing nonsensical things.

She got ready for bed and slid under the cool top sheet, hugging a pillow. She'd been half serious when she told Sarah she'd like to meet someone, but the other half of her wondered if it was a good idea. She'd spent so many years trying to convince her family and everyone else around her that she was responsible, and right now she felt as though she was throwing balls into the air and praying she could catch them all when they fell. Having a special someone to travel with would be nice, but it was a luxury that she couldn't afford at present.

9

"Okay, so the food order is taken care of, we've got tables and linens arranged, and the band is booked. How are the purchased auction items coming along?" Luke looked up from his list, his pen still touching the paper, ready to check off another box. His tall frame dwarfed the wrought iron chair he was sitting in at Donut Daze, Candle Beach's donut shop.

Charlotte sat back in her own chair and avoided eye contact with him. She really didn't want to tell him what she'd done or why she hadn't purchased the auction items they'd agreed upon.

"I can't buy the auction items."

"Didn't you order them already? Some of those bikes we decided on will take a while to get here." Luke stared at her.

A growing sense of dread filled her chest. She'd placed an order with a bike shop in Seattle for some mountain bikes to auction off at the fundraiser, but they'd called that morning to tell her that her credit card had been declined and they wouldn't be able to process the order.

"I had a problem with the order."

"What's going on? You said you'd take care of it." He set his pen down on the table and leaned forward.

"I can't pay for them," she said finally.

His head snapped back. "What do you mean you can't pay for them? I thought we were buying them with some of the funds that had already been donated."

"I spent that money already on decorations for the event." How had she been so stupid? Math had never been her strong suit and she'd somehow miscalculated what she'd already purchased. She'd figured she could put the bikes on her credit card and worry about how to pay for them later, but they must have gone over the limit.

His eyes widened. "You spent the money already? Charlotte—that's all the money we had. How are we going to pull this off now? Please tell me you already paid for the food for the dessert bar."

She squirmed in her chair and picked at the remains of the sprinkle donut on her plate. It crumbled beneath her fingertips.

"Uh." Tears were pushing at the insides of her eyes and she fought to hold them in. "I haven't done that yet." She leaned forward and rested her head in her hands, staring down at the table. Between long hours at the shop and painting in every moment of spare time she had, she'd let her fundraiser duties slide. Now it was coming back to bite her. She hated having to admit all of this to Luke, of all people.

"Hey," he said, touching her arm lightly. "What's going on?"

She looked up, the tears now flowing down her cheeks without a chance of stopping.

He froze, seemingly unable to take his eyes off her. "Are you okay?"

She nodded. "Yes." Then she broke down. "No. I don't know. I'm so sorry. I wanted to help Saul with this fundraiser, but it's too much. I've got the shop and an upcoming solo show at a gallery. I'm a little overwhelmed."

A smile crept across his face. "You've got a solo art show? That's fantastic. People are going to love your paintings."

She cocked her head to the side. "Have you seen my paintings?" Other than a couple of paintings she kept in the trailer for inspiration, she didn't usually show her art to people. To the best of her knowledge, Luke had never set foot in her trailer.

Now it was his turn to blush. "I saw them in your apartment that day I came to apologize for calling you Chatty Charlie. You had your easel set up in the living room and some canvases against the wall."

"Oh, right." She'd forgotten about that.

His eyes met hers. "You have talent. I wish I had some sort of artistic ability."

She couldn't do anything but stare at him, acutely aware that others in the crowded donut shop must think she was crazy for bursting into tears over her coffee and donut. Although she didn't see anyone staring at the moment, she'd probably have several friends that heard about her crying fit calling her later to ask if she was okay.

"Thanks." She looked down at the table. "But it doesn't really matter now. All people here in town will see is that I've completely screwed up this fundraiser."

"And why do you think they'd think that?" he asked.

"Because I screw everything up." She looked him straight in the eye. "Do you know what it's like to grow up a spoiled little brat who can't even take care of herself?"

His lips formed an *O*. "I didn't—"

She interrupted him. "Yeah, I know that's what you

thought of me—probably do still think of me. Chatty Charlie—all she knows how to do is spend money and chatter with her friends." She stood from the table and grabbed her plate. "Do you know how hard I've worked to get out from under my parents' money and try to figure out how to manage things on my own?"

He shook his head.

"Well apparently, I haven't done a very good job at learning how to manage money, because I got us into this mess!" She threw the paper plate in the trash and rushed out of the shop, afraid she'd burst into tears again in front of Luke. At least now she'd told him how she felt. It hadn't been until college that she'd realized how dependent she was on her parents and she'd been striving to prove herself ever since.

She left the donut shop and walked half a block down the hill, collapsing onto a wooden bench along the sidewalk. How had everything gone so wrong? She'd let everything going on in her life get to her and she'd completely messed up the fundraiser. Now Saul wouldn't get the help that he deserved and it was all her fault.

"Hey," Luke said as he slowly approached her. "Are you okay?"

She swiped at her eyes. "Oh sure, I'm fine. Can't you tell?"

He sat down next to her. "You don't look or sound fine."

She glared at him in response. "Just go away."

"Sorry, I can't do that. Parker would kill me if I left his little sister sitting here crying, alone on a bench."

"He probably wouldn't care. He's so busy with the new company and Gretchen—he never has any time for me."

"That's funny, he says the same thing about you." He tugged gently on her shoulder to make her face him.

Her lip quivered as she struggled to meet his gaze. Why was he being so nice to her?

"You're working yourself to the bone. So you messed up on the accounting for the fundraiser. So what? Give yourself a break."

"Easy for you to say, you didn't do it. I'm the one who ruined everything." She slumped against the bench, pressing the thick wooden slats into her back. "My parents were right. I'll never make it as an artist and I can't handle money. I probably should go back to working for them. Then I wouldn't have to worry about any of this."

He stared at her. "You don't mean that. Don't listen to your parents—they're wrong about you."

"No, they're not. I spent all of the money we had for the fundraiser and now it's ruined."

He sighed. "I can pay for the dessert bar and the bikes, okay?"

"What do you mean? Was there more money raised for the event?" Her spirits lifted. The fundraiser would be a success and she knew they'd recoup all of their costs. Everything she'd already spent money on would help increase the donations—of that, she was confident.

"Uh ... I've saved a bit of money from my old job."

"Even after buying the food truck? Those things can't be cheap. I spent everything I had on the Airstream for my shop and that's nothing compared to what a food truck must cost."

"Yeah, Charlotte. I have plenty of money. This is just a drop in the bucket and I don't mind donating it to the cause. If you give me the name of the bike shop, I'll call them later today and give them my payment information." He ran his feet along the ground in front of the bench and looked away, as if embarrassed to admit that he had money.

Gratitude rushed through her. She'd never expected having Luke Tisdale come back into her life would be a blessing instead of a curse.

She took a deep breath. "Thank you. I appreciate your generosity. And I swear I'll be more careful with the funds in the future."

"I'm sure you will." He smiled at her. "Don't worry about it. You've put a lot of effort into the fundraiser and it's going to be great. What did you buy anyway?"

"Some decorations."

He raised an eyebrow. "Just some decorations?"

"Oh, all right. I bought an antique picnic basket, some nice checkered cotton tablecloths, a few old-time photographs for the walls, and a few other things." She looked him in the eye. "I think they'll really make a difference for the event. There will probably be some big donors there and I want this to be a quality event."

He returned her gaze. "Okay. I trust you and your decorating abilities much more than my own. If you think those items were necessary, they probably were."

"Thank you." She smiled at him.

"Now, can we go over the list again?" He pulled his notebook and pen out of his pocket and set them on his lap.

She laughed. "Yeah, I think we can do that."

When they were through planning, they stood and walked together toward their shared parking lot. Luke watched her walking in front of him, her movements more subdued than normal. He'd never seen her so vulnerable. Usually she was bubbly and energetic, and he'd wondered if she was capable of being serious. When he knew her as a teenager, she'd been a spoiled brat, but she'd done some serious growing up over the years. She seemed to really care about the Bike Barn fundraiser and the people in this town.

They reached the lot, said a quick goodbye to each other that was encouragingly amicable and retreated to their own businesses. It was close to ten o'clock and although all the meats were already ready, he needed to get everything prepped for the lunch rush.

By lunchtime, he was mobbed, but as much as he tried, he couldn't concentrate on his customers. He somehow managed to mess up order after order and spent much of his time trying to fix his mistakes. Talking with Charlotte had really thrown him for a loop.

"I ordered the barbecued brisket, not the pulled pork." An elderly man wearing a fishing hat held up the food he'd just received from Luke.

Luke grabbed the paper boat piled high with shredded pork back from him. "Sorry about that, sir." He filled the order with the correct meat and stuck a cornbread muffin in a bag. "The muffin's on the house. Sorry for any inconvenience."

The man looked at him in surprise and smiled, any anger dissipated. "Thanks." He walked over to the bar seating that Luke had positioned against the back of the lot near the smoker.

The line for the food truck stretched past Charlotte's shop and out onto the sidewalk. His market research had been right. Candle Beach and its tourists loved barbecue. He looked past the waiting customers to Whimsical Delights.

Charlotte was sitting just inside the door on a high stool, sketching something on paper. She regarded the drawing, bit her lip, then erased whatever was bothering her. There was something charming about how focused she was when engrossed in her art, and he couldn't take his eyes off of her.

"Hey, man, I'd like to order," an impatient man in his twenties complained.

Luke flashed him a smile and snapped his attention back to his business. "Of course. What would you like?"

When the crowd had cleared, Luke found himself watching Charlotte again. This time, she was outside with an elderly woman, helping her choose a flamingo lawn statue. The woman finally selected a flamingo with a beach umbrella and Charlotte picked it up for her. As they walked into the Airstream, Charlotte cast a glance in his direction, then quickly turned her head away. Hopefully she wasn't worried about their interaction that morning being awkward. It had actually been endearing to see her in such an uncollected state.

He worked through the dinner crowd, then closed the service window at seven o'clock. By that time, customers were only trickling in and he'd had a long day. Over at the Airstream, Charlotte was picking up stray objects outside of her trailer and tidying the outdoor items.

Her hair hung over her shoulders as she picked up a lawn gnome and smiled at it, then patted it and stuck it back near the trailer door. He felt a wide grin creep across his face. Although she may have done a lot of growing up since they were kids, she hadn't lost the touch of whimsy that had always made people want to be her friend.

He'd been envious of that quality back then. Everything seemed to come to her easily, while he had to work for everything he got. Parker was the same way. They'd been friends, but Luke had always been partly jealous of how easy things were for the Gray kids. Now that he was older, he was coming to the realization that money didn't solve everything.

Before he could lose his nerve, he jumped down the truck steps and strode over to her.

"Hi," he said.

She looked up in surprise. "Hi. Did we have plans to work on the fundraiser tonight?"

"No. Actually, I was hoping you might want to come to dinner with me tonight. I've heard the Chinese restaurant is really good and I've been smelling barbecue all day, so it would be a welcome change."

He smiled at her. He hadn't been kidding about the barbecue smell. It had permeated every piece of clothing he owned, and although he loved the food he was getting a little sick of smelling like it. Soon he'd have to have a change of clothes ready to put on as soon as he came home so he could get a break from it.

She stared at him, not saying anything.

"Uh, or not." He'd thought they'd connected earlier, but he must have badly misjudged the situation. Even though Parker had given him the okay to date his sister, an unrequited interest would make things awkward for all of them. The silence between them was deafening. He started to back away.

"Wait. Do you mean like a date?" She toed the ground in front of her, smoothing out the line of crushed shells that formed a path to the entrance of her shop.

He looked up, afraid to hope.

"Yeah. Like a date."

She appeared to be considering it. "I don't know if that's a good idea." She gestured to their shared space. "I mean, we practically work together. And you're my brother's best friend."

"So?" He raised an eyebrow at her. "What about it?"

"So, things could get awkward between us." She picked up a female lawn gnome wearing a pink polka-dot skirt that was slightly out of place and pushed it firmly in line with the others.

"You mean more awkward than they already are?"

She laughed. "Yeah, good point. But still. What would Parker say?"

"He'd say go for it."

"Wait. Did you talk to him about me?" She put her hands on her hips and looked quite miffed.

"Umm ... Kind of."

She made a face. "I'm going to have to talk to my brother about butting into my love life."

"It wasn't like that. I asked him if you were seeing anyone because I wondered why you were so busy." He paused, thinking about his true motivation in speaking to Parker. "Okay, in hindsight, maybe it *was* a little like that."

"I have a lot of work to do for the art show and for the shop. That's why I'm so busy all of the time."

"I know. He told me that." He peered into her eyes. "So, what do you think? Would you like to go to dinner with me tonight?"

"No."

No? Had he been misreading the signs she'd exhibited in the last few minutes? He could have sworn she was flirting with him.

She laughed. "I have to get some work done tonight, but maybe a rain check? I probably could use a break from work."

"I'd like that." Had she just said yes to a date with him? A thought occurred to him. "Hey, do you want to play hooky from work and go hiking tomorrow after lunch? Things shouldn't be too busy on a Monday."

She turned to glance at her trailer, as if contemplating his suggestion. "I don't know. For a whole afternoon? I don't think I can take that much time off."

"Come on, it'll do you good," he wheedled. "You'll come back refreshed and ready to take on the world the next day. Maybe we can work on some of the plans for the fundraiser afterward too."

Her eyes searched his face. Finally, she spoke. "I guess I could do that. I do love to hike and I haven't been out much this summer. It stays light out until pretty late this time of year, so we should be fine if we leave in the afternoon. There are some nice trails around here."

"Great. Let's meet here at two thirty, okay?"

"Sounds good to me." She locked the door on the trailer and stuffed the key in her pocket. "I have to get going, but I'll see you tomorrow." She favored him with a sweet smile.

"See you then." He waited for her to round the corner onto Main Street and then uttered, "Yes!" out loud. Until then, he hadn't realized how much he cared about her and how badly he would have felt if she had completely rejected him. Now, all he had to do was to impress her with a perfect date. He could handle that, right?

10

─────────

"*A*re you ready?" Luke asked as he crossed from his side of the lot to hers. He had strapped his backpack on and changed into his hiking boots.

Charlotte glanced at him and smiled. "You look like you're ready to climb Mount Rainier."

"Is it too much?" he asked, gazing down at his clothes and pack.

She laughed. "No, you're good. It never hurts to be prepared." She looked ruefully down at the flowered sundress she wore. "I'm not ready though. I want to run home and change into something more appropriate for hiking. I didn't think about that when I got dressed this morning."

"No problem. I can wait for you here or walk over to your apartment with you."

"You can come with me," she said.

They walked next to each other, making awkward conversation. She wasn't sure why she'd accepted his invitation to go hiking with him. Even though he'd apologized profusely for the way he'd acted toward her in high school, he was still her brother's best friend.

When they reached the alley behind the bookstore, she opened the door and gestured to the stairs to her apartment. "Come upstairs if you'd like."

She didn't check to see if he was following her, but his footsteps sounded on the stairs behind her. After she let them in to her apartment, she disappeared into the bedroom and closed the door. When she came out dressed in a long-sleeve shirt over a tank top, long pants and hiking boots, she found Luke scrutinizing the paintings she'd leaned against every wall in the living room.

"These are wonderful," he said. "I didn't have a chance to see them very well before, so I'm glad I'm able to now. How long have you been painting?"

She stopped to think. It felt as though her art had always been an integral part of who she was, but the first time she'd picked up a paint brush and really tried to paint was in middle school. Her parents had worked long hours at their real estate company and she'd been home alone with her siblings every day after school in need of something to do.

"Since I was about thirteen." It was hard to believe she'd been painting for sixteen years already. "What about you? Do you have any artistic talents? Or play a musical instrument?"

"Well, I played the flute in high school because my grandmother thought I should." He grimaced. "I hated every minute of it."

She laughed. "Music has never been my thing either. I love listening to all types of it, but I'm tone deaf if I try to play an instrument or sing." She grabbed a backpack off the floor and gestured to the door. "Ready?"

He nodded and they walked down the stairs and outside.

"Where do you want to go?" he asked. "You've lived here longer, so you probably have a better idea of where to go."

"I do have a favorite place. The hike isn't too strenuous, but it's along the cliffs overlooking the water, just north of town."

"Sounds good. Do you want to drive since your car is here?"

"Sure."

They got into her car and she drove the few miles north to the trailhead on the west side of the highway. A few other people were parked there, but she found a spot in the small lot. A wood sign and an opening in the tree line indicated where the trail began.

They hefted their daypacks onto their backs and set out along the trail through a woodsy area. After a few minutes, they emerged from the trees at a lookout over the Pacific Ocean.

He walked over to the wooden safety rail and gripped it with his fingers, staring out at the horizon. "This is beautiful. I missed this so much."

She cocked her head to the side. "But you were living in San Francisco, right? It's gorgeous there too."

He shrugged. "Maybe, but I never had time to see anything of interest. The only places I ever saw were my office, my condo and the gym."

"Ugh," she said, gazing out over the water. With only a slight breeze, the breakers were small enough today for little kids to bodyboard on, and it looked like many families had taken advantage of the pleasant weather. "That sounds miserable."

Being outdoors was a huge part of her life, which probably explained her love of painting landscapes. There was nothing better than capturing a sunset over the Pacific with just the right shade of orange paint on a canvas.

He smiled. "It was."

Watching him at the railing, she realized how little she knew about him even though they'd known each other for so long.

"Do you have family around here?" she asked.

A shadow crossed his face. "It's just my Pops now. He and Grams raised me and my sister Zoe, who lives north of Seattle now."

"Oh." Although she sometimes hated having a big family living nearby, the thought of having hardly anyone around who was related to her was odd. "Are you close to your grandfather?"

He nodded. "Yes. He still lives in Haven Shores, although he moved into a retirement community after Grams passed."

She could tell from his voice that his grandparents were important to him. It was funny, she'd never really thought about Luke having a family before. It was as though in his role as Parker's friend, he was a one-dimensional caricature of a man. Now she was finding out what made him who he was.

She moved closer to the railing, standing just beyond touching as they stared out at the ocean together. She felt a connection between them, something that made her want to get closer to him. He looked over at her and smiled shyly. She looked up at him and returned the smile. He leaned closer to her, as though he was going to kiss her and her heart beat faster. Was this what she wanted?

He stepped back and took a sip from his water bottle. "Let's see what the rest of the trail looks like."

"Uh, sure." A sense of disappointment came over her. She *had* wanted him to kiss her, but now the moment had passed. Perhaps it was for the best though as any romance between the two of them could be sticky because of his life-long friendship with her brother. She'd hate to do anything to negatively affect that.

They walked side by side until the trail narrowed and they had to climb over a mass of gnarled tree roots to stay on the path. He walked in front of her and then held out his hand to help her over the roots.

She hesitated, then grasped his hand. Awareness zinged through her as their fingers touched and he pulled her to the other side, letting his hand linger against hers for a little longer than necessary.

"Thanks." She looked down at the ground, surprised by the intensity of her reaction to his touch. She'd had her share of boyfriends over the years, but never had the familiarity she felt now with Luke. A warmth spread over her. With their history, she wouldn't have believed they could work, but now she found herself wanting this date to go well.

"You're welcome." He flashed her a smile full of perfectly straight teeth.

The air was cooler as they moved into a more forested area of the trail. Charlotte looked up in appreciation at the canopy of trees heavy with green moss that dripped in tendrils from branches high overhead. The trees themselves were massive, with huge burrs that stuck out from the sides. She breathed in the mixture of salt air and rich earth that you could only find near the ocean.

"I really missed this," Luke said.

"All those years as a Boy Scout and you quit going

hiking. Tsk, tsk." She shook her head. "What would your scoutmaster say?"

Luke laughed. "He'd probably look at me in disappointment and say something like 'Young man, you need to get away from those electronics more often,' just like he did when I was a kid."

They reached the spot where Charlotte usually turned around.

"We'd better stop if we want to get back before it gets dark." She laughed. "Besides, I'm starving and I can't stop thinking about that Chinese food you mentioned yesterday."

"A woman after my own heart. I could eat too."

They retreated the way that they'd come, stopping at the overlook again to watch a man on the beach below throwing a stick for his dog. The dog leapt in the air to catch it, then ran jubilantly back to its owner. She closed her eyes for a moment, enjoying the warmth of the air, the sense of summer freeness, and the presence of the man beside her.

When she turned to move back onto the trail, her left foot caught on a tree root and she tumbled to the ground. Pain shot upwards from under her hiking boots.

"Charlotte!" Luke rushed over and knelt on the ground beside her. "Are you okay?" His eyes roved over her body, assessing her for any injuries.

"I think so." She pulled up the leg on her jeans, revealing some scraped patches of skin that stung as though she'd dipped them in a vat of turpentine.

"We'd better get you cleaned up." He threw his bag down on the ground and rifled through it until he found a small first aid kit. He pulled out an alcohol wipe and a large square Band-Aid. "This is going to hurt."

Charlotte grimaced. By this time her ankle was throbbing, but she didn't want to make a fuss.

He washed the wound with the alcohol wipe and applied the bandage, then looked at it with satisfaction. "Done." His attention moved to her face. "Are you okay? You're so pale."

She tried to force a smile on her face but failed. "It's my ankle."

He quickly unlaced her boot and pulled it and her sock off, revealing swollen flesh. He touched the injury and she winced.

"If you'd told me any later, we'd have had to cut the boot off."

"I didn't want to complain." Her excuse seemed lame now that she could see how bad her ankle looked.

He palpated the ankle, causing slivers of pain to shoot up her leg.

"Ah!" she yelped.

A look of horror came over his face. "Are you okay? I didn't mean to hurt you."

"I know." She sighed. "That hurt worse than I'd expected."

"I'm sorry." His eyes met hers. "Can you move your ankle at all?"

"I can try." She took a deep breath, then slowly rotated her foot while he held it above the ground. His fingers were warm on her flesh, but even his touch did little to soothe the pain.

He set her foot down on the ground with care and tugged the sock back up over her ankle. "I don't think it's broken, but in my non-expert medical opinion, you've got a pretty bad sprain."

She looked down the trail. "Now what? How am I going

to get back to the car?" Visions of a litter hauled by hulking men flashed through her head. This had to be the worst first date ever.

He assessed her gear. "Your pack looks pretty small. I think I can tuck it and your boot inside mine." He took care of that, then put the backpack on and looked down at her ankle. "Do you think you can stand if I help you up?"

She bent her right leg, leaving her injured left foot on the ground. "I think so."

He reached down and pulled her to a standing position. While holding her steady, he positioned himself beside her injured leg and hunched down slightly. "Put your arm over my shoulders."

She leaned in and wrapped her left arm over his shoulders and around his neck, and he gently grasped her hand with his left. He then reached his right arm across her waist from behind. Despite the pain in her ankle, the gentle pressure of his hand on her waist was very pleasant.

"Okay, now let's try this." He stood upright again, taking much of her weight himself, and nudged her forward as she hobbled along with him. "If you get tired I can carry you, but let's see how this works first."

"Okay." Her ankle still throbbed, but concentrating on moving forward, and his touch, helped her to focus on something other than the pain. Soon, she got into a rhythm of hopping on one foot as he continued to support much of her weight and kept her from falling. All that yoga she'd been practicing for years was coming in handy now to keep her balance.

"Do you want to stop?" His voice rang with concern.

"Uh, maybe for a minute."

He helped her to sit down on a log and she stretched her

right leg out and wiggled her foot. She wasn't used to hobbling on one leg.

"I think I'm ready to go now."

"Let me know if you need to stop again," he said. "But we're almost back to the trailhead."

She nodded and leaned against him again. He felt warm and solid with her arm around him. A few times she wobbled awkwardly while hopping along, and her free hand instinctively clasped over his hand around her waist in a slight panic. But every time his grip around her waist tightened ever so slightly to hold her steady, and she allowed her fingertips to linger for just a moment and lightly trace the back of his hand as she pulled hers away.

Finally, they were back at her car. He fished in her pack for the keys and unlocked the car, then opened the passenger door for her and lowered her to the seat. She winced as her ankle hit the side of the car as she moved her legs inside. Luke bent down to lift her leg and place it carefully inside.

"You need to get that looked at."

She wanted to protest but knew that he was right. It had been a wonderful first date, ending in the worst way imaginable.Spending the evening at the doctor's office probably wasn't what he'd had in mind for their date.

She sighed and said reluctantly, "The clinic in Candle Beach should still be open. You can drop me off there and I can call someone to pick me up when I'm done. I'm sure you have better things to do tonight." She peeked at him from under the doorframe, hoping he'd object to her offer.

He studied her face. "Are you kidding me? I'm not going to leave you there alone. What would Parker say if I left his injured little sister alone at the clinic? I'm pretty sure he'd want to beat the tar out of me."

She smiled faintly. He did care about her. "Well, I wouldn't want that to happen. I guess you'd better come with me."

He rested his hand on her shoulder, sending tingles down her spine. "I wouldn't have it any other way." He shut the car door and walked over to the driver's side, then drove her to the clinic to get checked out.

11

"These have to be the longest set of stairs I've ever seen." Charlotte stared up at her apartment from mid-flight. The stairs seemed to have grown since she'd last been there.

Luke laughed. "I'm pretty sure it's a normal staircase. Are you sure you don't want help going up?" He held up her crutches in one hand. "I've got an extra arm."

"No, I'm fine." She pulled herself up another step in an awkward hopping motion. Finally, they reached the top and Luke handed her the crutches.

He helped her to sit down on the couch with her leg outstretched and her foot on the coffee table.

She sighed. "Sorry, this wasn't a great date."

He smiled gently at her. "Don't worry about it. I had fun. Well, up until you got hurt."

"At least it's just a sprain. I should be off those things in a few days." She wrinkled her nose at the crutches he'd propped against the side of the couch within her reach.

"Do you need anything else? Maybe something to eat?" He hovered over her, making her unsettled.

He'd been so sweet to her the whole time after she'd been injured and in the Candle Beach Clinic. Although this date had definitely had its downsides, she didn't want it to end.

"I am still hungry. Maybe we could get takeout."

"Chinese?" he asked. "We never got our Chinese food."

"Perfect. We can eat Chinese food and watch a movie here." She peered up at him. "Would that work for you?"

"Fine with me. I didn't really want to leave you here right away without making sure you were going to be okay anyway."

They placed their takeout order with Lu's, and Luke went to get it when it was ready. On the way out, Alistair poked his head out from behind the couch and Luke waved a finger at him.

"I'm going to open this door slowly. Don't even think about making a break for it." He eased himself out the door and shut it behind him before the cat could follow.

Charlotte stifled a giggle at his overly exaggerated movements. "Alistair, come here." The cat ran to her and jumped up on the couch, rubbing his silky fur against her hand, then kneading her legs with his paws.

While he was gone, Charlotte flipped through the movie selections on the TV, settling on a romantic comedy she hadn't seen in years. After spending so much time with Luke that day and evening, the apartment seemed rather lonely with him gone. She hadn't realized how much time she'd spent by herself lately, with only Alistair for companionship.

A couple minutes later, she heard him come up the stairs.

"I've got rice, General Tso's, sweet and sour pork, and

broccoli beef," he announced. "Do you want to eat at the table or on the couch?"

She eyed the table. Too far. "Let's eat here." She patted the seat next to her. "Can you grab some plates out of the cupboard?"

He brought the food over to her and went back into the kitchen for plates and silverware.

"Did you find something to watch?"

"I did." She grinned. "How do you feel about eighties brat pack movies?"

"Uh, I hate to admit it, but I've never seen any."

"Ooh," she squealed. "You're missing out. We'll have to change that." Then she quieted. While the thought of watching many more movies with Luke appealed to her, she didn't know if she was being too presumptuous.

"I can't wait." He smiled and sat down next to her on the couch. His weight settling in on the old cushions caused her to fall toward him slightly. He put his arm against the back of the couch, almost touching her shoulders and she nonchalantly rested her head against his arm. Being this close to him, she was acutely aware of how much she was enjoying being with him.

They finished the Chinese food and the movie, then turned the TV off and leaned back against the couch cushions.

"What did you think?" she turned to him and asked. He'd appeared to be engrossed by the movie, but she hoped he hadn't been faking it.

"Of the movie?" He glanced at the blank TV. "I liked it. I'll have to rent some of the others you were talking about."

"I'd love to watch them again myself." She held her breath, waiting for him to accept her implied invitation for another movie date. When he said nothing, to hide her embarrassment, she said, "I'm starting to get tired." The adrenaline that had kept her going since spraining her ankle was wearing off.

"Do you want me to go?" He moved away from her and started to stand.

She didn't want him to leave and grabbed for his hand. "No. Wait."

He stopped. "Did you need something?"

"I was thinking about having a cup of coffee. Did you want one?"

"Sure."

"Can you help me to the kitchen?" she asked.

He reached his arm out and helped her hop over to the kitchen table, then busied himself with making a pot of coffee. Charlotte watched him expertly grinding the beans and filling the reservoir with water. *I could get used to this*, she thought. It had been a long time since she'd been on a date or had a man in her apartment, but she was enjoying having him around.

He sat down at the table while they waited for the coffee to brew.

"How long have you lived here?" he asked, looking around.

"About eight months. I used to live in Gretchen's house when I first moved to Candle Beach, and before that, in an apartment in Haven Shores."

"Do you like it here?"

"I love it." Joy rushed through her. "I can't even remember what it was like to live anywhere else. The people here are so nice and I've made friends that I know I can count on. That's something you don't find else-where." She looked at him. "What about you? Are you liking it here? It must be a big change from San Francisco."

"It is, but I'm enjoying it. Things there didn't seem quite real, almost like I was living someone else's life. Having the food truck and producing something that people enjoy has been life changing."

"Wow. That's a big endorsement for the positive effects of owning a food truck."

He shrugged. "It's true. I love what I do."

He stood to pour coffee for them and set a cup in front of her.

"Thanks," she said, wrapping her hands around the cup.

They talked for a while longer about his plans for the food truck, and her art, then he stood to go. She pulled out her crutches and stood too, leaning against the kitchen table with her left foot hovering above the linoleum floor.

"I had a nice time," he said.

"Minus the visit to the clinic?" she teased.

"Yeah, besides that." He moved closer to her and her breath caught.

Was he going to kiss her? Her heart beat faster as she waited for him to make a move. He reached for her, then leaned down and kissed her—on the cheek.

She fought the urge to scream. The date had been going well, so what had happened? Had he changed his mind about her? Was this because she was Parker's little sister? She'd finally found someone that she liked, and who was interested in her, and now she'd just been pushed back into the friend zone.

He stepped back. "Did I do something wrong?"

Yes? No? She didn't know what to say. Fine. She was just going to have to call him out on it.

"Is it because I'm Parker's sister?"

NICOLE ELLIS

"Is what?"

"The reason my goodnight kiss became a peck on the cheek?" Heat rose under the collar of her long-sleeve shirt, but she wasn't backing down now. She met his gaze head-on.

His smiled at her. "Not at all. I was trying to be polite, this being our first date and all."

She sighed. She didn't want to have to wait to see if she'd imagined their chemistry after all these years. "Try again."

This time, he leaned in and let his lips graze hers ever so slightly, but stayed there, tantalizing her for a few seconds. When he moved away, she took a deep breath and fought to gain control of her emotions.

"Better?" he asked with a gleam in his eyes.

She smiled. "Yeah, that was a little better. But you'll have to try harder next time."

"Oh, I will." He stepped backward, narrowly missing Alistair, who'd decided he liked Luke and was trying to rub against his legs. "I'll see you tomorrow."

He locked the door from the inside and left. Charlotte lowered herself down to the kitchen chair she'd been sitting in before and touched her lips. They still tingled from the kiss.

"Oh, he's going to be trouble," she said to Alistair, who promptly ignored her and ran off into the bedroom. She sat there for a while, replaying their date. Luke had surprised her. He'd been kind and patient with her after she was injured, but he had a sense of play in him that she hadn't anticipated. Unlike most of the men she'd dated, she could see a future with him, and she couldn't wait to see where things went.

The Bluebonnet Café was busy when Luke stopped by to pick up some coffee and pastries to bring to Charlotte at the lot. Charlotte's friend Angel was manning the cash register. When he and Charlotte had met for a lunch date earlier in the week, she'd introduced him to her friend, who'd then joined them for lunch.

When it was finally his turn, the line had died down and Angel greeted him warmly. "Hey, Luke."

"Hi, Angel." He leaned against the counter and scanned the selection of pastries in the glass bakery case. "What's good today?"

"I recommend the cherry Danishes," a voice from behind him said.

Angel blushed. "Of course you do," she said to the man in a teasing voice. Then she turned back to Luke. "That's my boyfriend, Adam. He's a Danish-aholic. He's rarely far from a pastry."

Adam shot her a faux scathing glare. "Hey, that's not fair. This time I'm here so we can go for a walk on your break." He eyed the baked goods. "Although I could use another donut."

Angel grinned. "So, what can I get for you?"

Luke laughed. "The Danishes do look tasty. I think I'll take two cherry Danishes and two of those blueberry muffins, along with two cups of coffee."

"Ah," she said knowingly. "Are you bringing Charlotte breakfast?"

He nodded.

"That's so nice of you," she said as she slid his credit card into the chip reader.

"Well, it's the least I could do after she got injured when we were out hiking together. It's hard for her to get around, although she's been doing better every day." He thought back to their first date. It had been a day of strong emotions. He'd wanted to kiss her while they were looking out at the ocean, but he'd chickened out and missed his moment. Then, she'd fallen on the trail and hurt herself. Seeing her in pain had been horrifying and he'd known then how much he cared for her. He'd thought the date was ruined, but they'd salvaged it. And that kiss they'd shared right before he'd left—that had been magical.

"Hey, here's your food." Angel gave him an odd look that told him he'd been daydreaming for too long. She handed him two cups of coffee and his pastries. "Tell her *hi* from me, okay?"

"I will."

Angel had already greeted a customer that had come in and was taking his order.

Before he could walk out the door, Adam stopped him. "Thanks for volunteering to help with the fundraiser. It means a lot to this town."

"No problem. I'm glad to help. This is my town now too."

Adam nodded. "Charlotte's been canvassing everyone in town for donations." He laughed. "She's a hard bargainer. I offered to donate a half-page ad in the paper to advertise the event and she somehow talked me into a full-page ad and a monetary donation."

Luke raised an eyebrow. "Impressive. Thanks for the donation."

"Of course," Adam smiled. "This town has stuck by me too. It wasn't too long ago that I was having some financial problems with the newspaper, but Angel and some of her friends figured out a way to save the paper. It's been running continuously for over a hundred years, and it would have killed me to shut it down."

"That's amazing." He felt surer than ever that starting his

own business in Candle Beach had been the best decision he'd ever made. He held up the cardboard coffee carrier. "I'd better get these to Charlotte before they're cold, but thanks again for the donation."

Adam gave him a little wave. "Enjoy the Danishes."

12

A week and a half later, Charlotte had business in Haven Shores. Her ankle was still bothering her, so Luke drove her there. She'd had him drive her to the big box store, but she hadn't told him what she was picking up.

"What are you getting there anyway?" he asked as he drove south on the highway to Haven Shores.

"I ordered a new computer for Whimsical Delights. My old one is dying. They were able to get me a good discount on it in the store versus what I'd pay online, so I ordered through them."

"Okay. So, we'll pick up your computer and then maybe go eat somewhere?"

She nodded. "Sounds good." She twisted in the passenger seat to talk to him. "I'm so excited about this computer. It'll make ordering new inventory and paying bills a snap. My old computer is so slow."

"It's surprising all of the things you need for a small business." He'd been astounded at how many things he'd had to buy for his business that he hadn't anticipated. The desk in his studio apartment was looking more crowded with each day that passed.

He drove into the parking lot of the office supply store and parked near the door.

"Do you want me to come in with you?" he asked.

"Nope, this shouldn't take too long." She eased herself out of the car and limped slightly as she walked into the store. She hadn't used her crutches in a few days, but the ankle injury was obviously still bothering her.

He rolled down the windows and rested his arm along the car door. A soft breeze blew through the parking lot, so although the temperature was in the eighties that afternoon, it was quite pleasant. After a while, he found himself tapping his fingers against the side of the car. Where was she? She'd been gone for at least thirty minutes already.

He rolled the windows up and got out of the car, stretching his legs before entering the store. He found her at the back, talking with the salesperson.

"Hey," he said as he came up behind her and put his arm on her back. "What's going on?" He looked between her and the salesperson, noticing the laptop box on the counter.

The salesperson said nothing, and just looked at Charlotte.

She flushed crimson. "I was checking out the computer and then I discovered that my credit cards aren't working. I forgot I'd bought those decorations on my card and I left my checkbook at home. I'm trying to figure out how I can get back down here to buy the laptop."

He didn't say anything for a moment. The forgotten checkbook bit was a little too familiar to him, although the women he'd dated had usually used it for little trinkets or other things they'd picked up while out on a date with him.

A computer was a big purchase. However, she wasn't like the other women he'd dated.

He pulled his credit card out of his wallet and swiped it through the credit card reader. Almost immediately, the cash register spat out a slip of paper for him to sign. He signed with a flourish and then pushed it across the counter.

"Thank you, sir," the clerk said, handing him the receipt and the laptop box, which he'd placed in a large plastic bag.

Charlotte stared at him openmouthed. "You didn't have to do that. I didn't ask you to do that."

He couldn't tell by her tone if she was happy or upset that he'd helped.

"No problem." He smiled at her. Had he made the right decision? He'd acted without thinking and this was a big-ticket item.

"I promise I'll pay you back." She held up three fingers. "Scout's honor."

A smile broke through his concern. He and Parker had been Eagle Scouts together and Charlotte had been required to attend way too many badge ceremonies when they were kids. He wanted to think the best of her, but a little part of him remembered how she'd been as a teenager who'd lived to spend her parents' money. He didn't want her to think of him as nothing but a piggy bank.

She took a deep breath. Her expression was conflicted at first, but then a look of relief crossed her face. "Thank you. I swear, I'll pay you back as soon as we get home."

He took her hand and squeezed it. "I'm not worried."

She nodded.

"Did you have someplace in mind for dinner?" he asked as they got into the car.

"Nope, you?"

"I was thinking Arturo's if that's okay with you. I've

heard great things about it from Parker and I haven't had a chance to try it out yet."

She didn't say anything at first. Then she said, "Arturo's is awfully pricey. Maybe we could go somewhere else?"

"Oh, don't worry, it's my treat. Besides, you don't have any money with you, remember?" he teased.

"I remember." She looked away. "I just think I'm in the mood for Mexican food. What do you think about going to Papa Tito's?"

"That place is still around?" He laughed. "I've been going there since I was a kid. Pops always loved eating there."

She looked up at him. "You know, I haven't met your grandfather yet. What do you think about inviting him to come with us?"

It wasn't exactly the romantic date he'd expected, but she'd just asked to meet his grandfather, one of the most important people in his life, and he couldn't turn down that opportunity.

"Sure. Let me give him a call to see if he's around."

He pulled out his phone and dialed.

"Hey, Pops."

"Luke," his grandfather said warmly. "I've been meaning to call you. I had the best poker game last night. I won fifty bucks off Henry Olsen."

Luke laughed. "That's great that you won last night. Say, Charlotte and I were here in Haven Shores and we were wondering if you'd like to come to dinner with us at Papa Tito's."

"Oh, that Charlotte?" Pops teased him.

He sighed. "Yes, that Charlotte. She really wants to meet you."

"Well in that case, I'd love to come. Do you mind picking me up?"

"We'll be there in about five minutes. See you, Pops."

Charlotte smiled at him as he finished his conversation.

He hung up. "Pops said he'd love to come to dinner and meet you. If you don't mind, he'd like for us to pick him up at home."

"Of course."

They drove to the retirement home, which had been built just beyond the dunes a few blocks away from the main drag through town.

"Wasn't there an old hotel here before?" Charlotte asked as they got out of the car and walked toward the front door of the building.

"Yes. They tore it down about ten years ago to build the retirement home."

"I guess I don't get over to this area much anymore." She peered at the facility. "It's beautiful."

The retirement home looked like a nice hotel, with two offset wings so that each apartment had individual balconies looking out over the water. Luke had always found them to take good care of the building and, most importantly, his grandfather seemed happy there.

"Pops has a one-bedroom apartment on the third floor." He opened the door to the retirement home and motioned for her to enter in front of him.

They walked into the lobby and were greeted by a woman at the front desk. Luke then led Charlotte into an elevator, which let them out onto a carpeted hallway.

She suddenly felt nervous. She'd suggested inviting Pops

because she knew Luke was close to him and they were in the area already, but she hadn't considered the implications. This was like meeting the parents in Luke's situation. Was it too soon in their relationship to meet Pops? If it was, it was too late to change her mind.

He stopped at a door midway down the hall and knocked.

"Coming," an elderly man called out. He opened the door and smiled at Luke, then beamed at Charlotte. "This must be the famous Charlotte."

"Pops!" Luke said. "She's going to think I talk about her all the time."

"You do." Pops grinned widely at Charlotte. "It's nice to meet you. You can call me Pops too."

"Nice to meet you, Pops." She relaxed a little. He was anything but intimidating as he led them into a bright, sunlit apartment and gestured to the couch.

"Have a seat," he said. "Let's chat for a bit before we go to dinner."

They sat dutifully and he sat back in a chair across from them.

"So, Charlotte, you're Parker's sister."

She nodded. "Yes."

He laughed. "I hope you're not getting him into trouble as much as Parker used to do when they were kids."

At that, she burst out laughing. "They were always in trouble, weren't they?"

"Pops," Luke admonished him. "Be nice."

His grandfather waved his hand in the air. "I am being nice. But I want to get to know this young lady." He peered at her. "Your parents are still here in town, right? Did you go into the family business like your brother?"

"No, sir. I own a gift shop in Candle Beach."

"Charlotte's a wonderful artist too," Luke said. "She has a beautiful painting of the ocean at sunset."

"That's great." Pops smiled at her. "You know, Luke's grandmother was quite an artist too." He pointed at an oil painting of a sailboat behind him. "That's one of hers."

"It's beautiful," Charlotte said truthfully. She rose to inspect it more closely. "I like how she captured the wind in the sails."

Pops nodded. "She loved painting." A look of sadness crossed his face, then he clapped his hands on his knees and pushed himself off of the chair. "Well, enough chit-chat, let's go eat."

They drove to Papa Tito's, where Charlotte and Luke sat across from Pops at a booth.

"It's been a while since I've been here." Luke perused the menu. "But, I think I'm going to get the taco platter, just like I always used to do."

"Me too," Pops said. "Your grandmother always got the stuffed peppers and I thought she was crazy. That woman loved spicy food." He drank from his water glass.

"I used to come here with friends from work after I moved back to Haven Shores after college." Charlotte closed her menu and set it on the table. "I always get the same thing, I don't know why I even bother looking at the menu."

The waitress came and took their order and they ate their fill of tortilla chips while they waited.

"Better than Arturo's?" Luke asked Charlotte.

She shrugged. "I've never been there, but this sounded good." And cheaper, she thought. Even though she knew Luke could afford a more expensive meal, she didn't want him to think she was taking advantage of him, especially after the fiasco with the computer.

The waitress brought their food and they dug in. Luke and his grandfather quickly finished their tacos and chatted while she was still working on her Arroz Con Pollo.

"So, how's business at the truck?" Pops asked.

Luke grabbed a chip out of the basket in the middle of the table. "Business is good. I'm glad I came back to the coast. With all the tourist traffic, Candle Beach was the right choice for a barbecue place."

"I'm glad you're back too." Pops' eyes fell to the table. "I wish your sister would come home. I miss her."

Luke reached his hand across the table and rested it on the old man's hand. "I know. But she seems happy in Willa Bay. She's doing what she always wanted to do. Remember how frequently her Barbie and Ken dolls got married?" He shook his head. "We should have known she'd have a future in wedding coordination."

Charlotte set her fork down. "Do you think Zoe will stay in Willa Bay?" She hadn't known Zoe well in school as Luke and his sister were a few years older, but she remembered seeing her around.

Luke glanced at his grandfather. "I think she'll stay there, at least for the near future. It's the wedding capital of the Northwest, so her services are in high demand."

"Hmm," Charlotte said as she swirled her fork through her Mexican rice. "I've never been there before, but I've seen the pictures of the tulip fields. It's a beautiful part of the state."

Pops gave her a shrewd look. "But not as beautiful as the coast. You'll never find a better place to live than here. And I'm hoping I'll someday get to see my great-grandchildren enjoying the same beach I grew up on." He eyed Luke, then returned his gaze to her.

Charlotte smothered a grin at his implication. She'd been nervous about meeting Luke's grandfather, but she'd seemed to have won him over. She swallowed the last bite of her food.

"Do you want to come with us for a walk along the boardwalk?" she asked Pops.

"Oh no," he demurred. "I've got to get back to the retirement home. Henry Olsen has a poker game starting at seven, and I intend to beat him again tonight."

"Are you sure?" Luke asked.

"Of course, I'm sure." Pops winked at him and Charlotte tried to keep from laughing again. She wished her own grandfathers had been half as fun as Pops.

"Well, don't let us keep you," Luke said. "I'd hate for Henry Olsen to get the upper hand." The check came and he paid it.

After they waved goodbye to Pops outside the retirement home, Charlotte felt full, both from food and from the happiness that comes from a meal with good company. She'd been unsure what Pops would be like, but he was as wonderful of a man as Luke had made him out to be. She only hoped that she could live up to any good things that Luke had told Pops about her.

The meeting between Charlotte and his grandfather had gone even better than Luke had hoped. The old man had taken him aside while she was in the restroom and told him that she was a keeper. He'd even gone so far as to hint that she'd make a great mother. Luke had tried to shush him before Charlotte returned, but Pops had managed to get a few comments in about what a great grandson Luke was to him. Charlotte had taken it in stride, smiling and nodding at everything Pops said.

After they dropped his grandfather off at home, they left the car parked in front of the retirement home and walked the few blocks back to town to get ice cream. On a Thursday night, it wasn't too crowded. They received their cones quickly and took them out to the boardwalk.

When they passed by Arturo's, Luke gestured to it. "I do want to try this place out though. Parker raves about it. It looks like they're doing good business tonight."

"Gretchen told me it was good too," Charlotte said. "I bet you look at things differently now that you own a restaurant of sorts."

Luke laughed. "Too true. I find myself wondering about what their profit margins are or what marks they received on their last health code inspection, and assessing the menu options to determine if I need to add something new to my own offerings. However, I've tried to avoid the barbecue place here in town so that I don't end up stealing one of their ideas inadvertently."

Charlotte glanced up at him. "But isn't it good business sense to know what the competition is up to?"

"Well, yes, it is. But it's so much more than just a business to me. I put something of myself into each new menu item that I try. I don't want to lose that by just responding to the competition."

They walked past the restaurant, licking their cones before the ice cream melted down the sides.

"As an artist, I can appreciate the desire for self-expression. But how did you end up buying a barbecue food truck, anyway?" Charlotte asked. "If I'd earned a lot of money selling stock, I think I'd retire. Well, maybe not."

He sighed. "It came down to me hating my job. And I

mean hating—like in a really unhealthy way. I dreaded going to work, but being a software developer was all I'd ever done and it's hard to pass up the salary I was earning."

"But why barbecue?"

"Why not?" He smiled. "It's my favorite food. Plus, there was a barbecue food truck that parked just down the street from my office and I struck up a conversation one day with the owner. He agreed to take me under his wing and I just went from there. When it came time to sell my stock, I cashed out and bought the truck. Finding a place to park it was the hard part."

"And you just had to park it next to Whimsical Delights."

"Yes." He smirked. "It was all part of a devious plan to see you again and annoy you into dating me."

She looked at him. "You are kidding, right?"

"Of course I am!" He chuckled. "I had no idea you even lived in Candle Beach. I would have pegged you as someone who'd leave town for the big city and never look back."

A darkness crossed her face and he sobered. He'd accidentally struck a nerve.

"Sorry," he said quickly.

"It's okay. Honestly, I never thought I'd be back either, but something pulled me back." She shrugged. "When I lived away from the coast, it was like something was blocking me from fully expressing myself through my art. Being by the ocean frees me." She gazed out at the waves crashing on the wet sand.

"I know what you mean," he said. "I feel the same way."

"When I decided to open my shop, I chose Candle Beach. It seemed to have good tourist traffic and it was far enough away from most of my family, but still close to home." She grimaced. "It took me far too long to earn the money to buy the Airstream though. I thought I'd never get away from working for my parents."

"So there was never any thought of you going into the family business?" He bit into the waffle cone, the delicious vanilla-flavored confection crunching between his teeth.

She shook her head vigorously. "No, never. That was for Graham and Parker. Not my thing. But telling my parents that wasn't easy. They're proud of what they've attained and they think we should all follow in their footsteps."

"That's funny, because my grandparents wanted me to get out of town and do something other than the restaurant business, and here I am."

They walked onto the beach, finishing their ice cream cones before they reached the water. The tide was out and the beach seemed to stretch on forever. The water licked at their feet as they walked along the hard-packed sand.

Luke pulled his shoes off and tossed them onto dry sand, then walked into the water.

"What are you doing?" Charlotte asked.

"I'm washing off my hands. They're covered in ice cream." He grinned at her and scooped up a handful of water, then threw it at her.

"Why you ..." She kicked off her sandals and followed him into the water, laughing.

They splashed each other until they were both soaked. She should have looked like a drowned rat, but he'd never seen a more beautiful woman. Her glowing smile reached all the way to her eyes and her laughter made his heart sing.

He stood still for a moment, taking it all in.

"Now what are we going to do?" Charlotte asked, pulling her wet clothes away from her body.

NICOLE ELLIS

"Eh, we'll dry off." He reached for her hands and held them out to the sides, stepping forward until their bodies were touching.

She smiled and brushed a lock of wet hair off his forehead with her fingers, then wrapped her arms around his neck. Droplets of water dripped from her hair onto his arms as he pulled her tightly against him. The water provided a cool contrast to the heat he felt rising inside.

He tipped his head down to kiss her. She tasted of cherries and vanilla ice cream, an intoxicating combination that made him want more. She sighed and kissed him deeper, threading her fingers through his hair, sending tingling sensations through his scalp.

He pulled away slightly so he could see her face. Her cheeks were bright from the saltwater and sun, and her eyes were half-closed. He'd never seen anyone as enchanting as she was, standing there in front of him without makeup, soaking wet and hair tangled from the wind.

"Luke," she murmured, moving closer to him. He stood there, inhaling her scent, never wanting to forget such a perfect moment.

Water swirled around their feet, but they didn't move until Charlotte called out, "Our shoes!"

He looked behind them to see her sandal being lifted off the sand by a wave. He broke apart from her and ran over to it, nabbing the shoe before the ocean could wash it away.

"You saved it!" Laughing, she waded through the water to pick up her other sandal. Her hair swayed as she walked, sunlight glinting through it like slivers of gold. He forced himself to look away and picked up his own shoes before the water hit them too.

She shivered, clutching her sandals to her chest.

"I think we'd better dry off now." He took her hand and

led her up to the dry sand, where they sat next to a beach log to let the waning sun warm their wet clothes. She snuggled close to him and they chatted for a while, making up stories about the other beachgoers until they were ready to go home. He couldn't have asked for a more romantic date.

13

*C*harlotte looked longingly at her art supplies. The art show was in two days and she needed to take her paintings to Seattle, but all she wanted to do was paint. She'd invited Angel to tag along on the road trip, and they planned to shop for dresses for Maggie and Jake's upcoming wedding while they were in the city. She'd recently hired a local teenager to work at Whimsical Delights part-time for the summer so she could have some much-needed time off, but now she was second-guessing her decision to spend a whole day away from the business.

A knock sounded at her apartment door, jarring her away from her thoughts.

"It's unlocked!" she called out.

Angel poked her head in. "Are you ready?"

Charlotte glanced around the room. Did she have everything? Keys, check. Purse with wallet, check. The last time she'd been away from something resembling work for more than a few hours had been so long ago that she couldn't even remember it. It was probably time for a break if she wanted to avoid the burnout she'd seen some of her friends go through as they pursued their careers.

She grinned at Angel. "I am. We're going to stop for coffee though, right?"

"Of course." Angel laughed. "And I made a playlist of songs to keep us company on the way to Seattle. I'm so excited! I love Candle Beach, but after living in Los Angeles for so long, being in a small town makes me feel a little claustrophobic if I don't get out of here once in a while."

They made their way outside to Charlotte's car parked across the street. At this time of year, the tourist portion of the parking lot was almost full, even early in the morning. Good thing she had a reserved parking spot, although she wouldn't be too surprised to find a tourist blocking her spot when she and Angel returned that evening.

"It's a beautiful day too." Charlotte gazed upward as she stuffed her purse in the back seat. A few puffy marshmallow clouds dotted the brilliant blue sky. "Days like this make me wish I had my convertible back."

"You had a convertible? In Washington?" Angel smiled. "You don't see too many of those here like you do back in Southern California."

"I may have been a little spoiled as a teenager," Charlotte admitted. "My parents bought me one when I turned sixteen."

"Uh, yeah. I'd say so." Angel situated herself in the car and pulled the seatbelt across herself. "So, why'd you get rid of it?"

Charlotte shrugged. "When I graduated from college I decided I wanted to make it on my own and the insurance was too expensive. I sold it and bought an old beater that I drove for a while until I could afford this one." She tightened her fingers around the steering wheel of the used Honda Accord she'd purchased a few years ago from the money she'd earned at her parents' real estate company.

"I can't even imagine," Angel said. "When I was a teenager, it was just me and my mom, and she barely had enough money left at the end of the month to feed us, much less buy me a car."

"Having money had its pluses and minuses. I never had any money insecurities, but my mother wasn't the easiest person to live with. I envy the close relationship you had with your mother." Her mother hadn't been bad, but she'd been distant for much of Charlotte's life.

"I know. I was lucky," Angel said wistfully. "I miss her."

"Oh, I'm sorry, I didn't mean to upset you," Charlotte said, suddenly feeling horrible for reminding Angel of her mother's death that year.

"It's okay." Angel smiled. "I think about her all the time and living in Candle Beach now where she grew up has made me feel even closer to her."

Angel's words held a hint of sadness, so Charlotte flipped on the air conditioner and changed the subject. "It's getting warm already."

"It is." Angel turned in her seat, drilling her eyes into Charlotte. "So how are things going with Luke?"

Heat rose up her neck. "It's only been about two weeks, so it's still fairly new."

"Okay, spill. I saw the way you looked at him when we had lunch. Everyone quizzed me when I started dating Adam, now it's my turn."

Charlotte sighed. "It's kind of weird."

"Weird how?"

"Luke is Parker's best friend from high school."

"Seriously? You didn't tell me that before. You're a walking cliché."

"I know. And in high school I hated him, but now ..."

"Now he's so dreamy you can't stay away from him?"

Charlotte took her eyes off the road for a second and mock-glared at Angel. "No, but he's changed. He's so sweet and kind to me." Her heart surged with happiness thinking of Luke and how he made her feel like she could do anything. Unbidden thoughts of how he'd come to her rescue with the computer floated into her mind, competing with the happy memories. Even though she'd paid him back as soon as they'd returned from Haven Shores, she felt conflicted about how easy it had been for him to whip out his credit card to pay. "Although, there are some things about him that I'm not sure about."

"Like what?"

Charlotte could feel Angel's eyes drilling into her face.

"Like the fact that he's probably a millionaire several times over and I don't want to fall back into the trap of letting someone pay for things for me."

"Whoa. You're upset that he has money?" Angel laughed. "If someone wanted to buy me things, I don't think I'd complain."

Charlotte leaned her head against the headrest as she drove on a straight stretch of highway. "I know. It's ridiculous and illogical, but I can't help how I feel. He's such a great guy and I wish I could get over the money thing. Money always complicates everything."

"Hmm," Angel said. "Well, I'm sure you'll figure it out. I'm sure you're different than you were back then. And if he's Parker's best friend, he can't be that bad, right? Has Gretchen met him?"

NICOLE ELLIS

Charlotte nodded. "Yes. She thinks I'm crazy to not be so smitten with him that I forget my fears about money." She turned off the highway onto the main freeway to Seattle. "Can we talk about something else?"

"Sure." Angel turned the air conditioning up a notch. "What kind of dress are you looking for? A sundress, or something more formal?"

"Something in between. My budget for a dress isn't huge, but I'll know it when I see it."

"Okay," Angel said. "Hey, are you excited about your art show?"

"I am."

Charlotte's stomach churned thinking of everything she still had left to do to prepare for it. Maybe taking a day off hadn't been the best of ideas, but a shopping trip with Angel had sounded like fun when she'd originally committed to it.

"I can't even imagine how thrilling it must be." Angel sighed. "That's so cool that you'll get to show everyone your art."

"You'll get your chance to shine. Have you thought about opening your own bakery?"

Angel recoiled. "Oh no, I couldn't do that to Maggie. She was so kind to give me the job at the café."

"I don't think she'd mind. You know Maggie—she's always encouraging everyone to go after their dreams."

"True." Angel looked out the window. "I don't know. I'll talk to her about it."

"Good."

They drove until they reached the gallery in downtown Seattle. Charlotte parked in the alley behind the gallery to unload her paintings.

"Are you sure it's okay to park here?" Angel asked, staring out the window at the dark alley.

"Raymond told me to park here and then come find him inside." She and Angel got out of the car and approached the front side of the old brick building.

"This place is beautiful," Angel said as she admired the exterior.

"So's the inside." Charlotte opened the door to reveal a large open room with two-story high ceilings, white-washed walls, and cement floors. The building had an industrial feel that didn't try to compete with the artwork on display.

"Do you mind if I look around while you find the owner?" Angel asked. "Those sculptures are breathtaking."

Charlotte laughed. "Nope, go ahead." She left Angel in the entry to the gallery and walked through the large main room into another side room.

"Ah, Charlotte, you made it," Raymond Donohue said from across the room as she came around the corner.

She pasted a bright smile on her face, hoping to counteract the butterflies that were dancing around in her stomach. This was really happening.

"I did." She walked purposefully over to him. "I have everything in my car outside.

"Well, then, let's take a look, shall we?" He led her to a door leading to the back alley where she'd parked her car. He had an assistant carry in the artwork and lean them against the walls. After he'd removed the coverings, he stepped back. "Charlotte, they're gorgeous."

She let out her breath. "Thank you." She'd brought a selection of paintings that she felt best represented Candle Beach, the place that she'd come to call home. There were several canvases of sunsets over the water, a few of boats in the marina and the painting she'd done of Bluebonnet Lake. "Is there anything else you need from me?"

He smiled at her. "No, only your presence at the opening. You will be there, right?"

"I wouldn't miss it for the world." The butterflies were moving around now like they were caught in a tornado. She'd be lucky to get out of there without hyperventilating.

"Fantastic. I'll see you then." He left, slipping quietly into another room. She walked back to the main gallery and found Angel gazing at a six foot tall sculpture of a woman and child.

"It's so beautiful." Angel turned to Charlotte and did a double take. "Are you okay? You're so pale."

Charlotte took several calming breaths. "I'm fine, just a little overwhelmed by it all."

"I can see why," Angel said. "This place is amazing. I wish I could go to your show, but I have to work."

"I know. But thank you for coming with me today." Charlotte's nerves eased and she was able to talk without feeling as though someone were squeezing out her insides. "Now, let's go find dresses for the wedding."

They drove to a large shopping mall just out of the city. Several department stores anchored the corners of the mall and shops were crowded around the exterior as well.

Angel's eyes widened. "This is huge."

"Yep." Charlotte smiled. "Let's get to it. We only have a few hours before we should get going back to Candle Beach if we want to get home at a decent hour."

"You don't have to tell me twice." Angel hopped out of the car and they walked in the entrance of a large department store.

Later, exhausted after working their way through the mall, Charlotte had found an inexpensive but nice-looking flowered sundress to wear to the wedding and Angel had found a sleeveless shift with metallic designs on navy-blue fabric.

They arrived home to Candle Beach too late for Charlotte to paint, but she didn't mind. They'd had a good time and it seemed to have been just what she needed, because for the first time in weeks, her head was clearer and she didn't feel the stress of her commitments.

14

The next day, Charlotte had big plans for celebrating the Fourth of July with Luke. She loved the holiday and couldn't wait to take him to one of her favorite places in the area to watch the fireworks.

"Where are you taking me?" Luke asked as she tied a blindfold behind his head.

She laughed. "If I told you, then I would have to kill you."

"Oh, that serious?" he teased. "Wherever we're going had better live up to the hype."

"It will," she said mysteriously. "You'll see."

She helped him into the passenger side of her car and closed the door behind him. Easing the car onto the road, she couldn't help but smile at herself a little. Luke would enjoy this.

"You know, I can't help feeling like I'm being kidnapped," he quipped.

"Oh," she exclaimed with mock surprise. "You don't care for blindfolds?"

"No, it's just that you could be taking me pretty much

anywhere. A dark alley, an old abandoned warehouse, a secluded spot way out in the woods—it wouldn't be hard to hold me for ransom. How well do I really know you, anyway?"

She stole a glance at him, shocked at the implication, but then she noticed his playful smile. *I knew he was joking. Why does the reminder of his money make me second-guess myself?*

"Anyway, not everyone is blessed with such a stunningly beautiful kidnapper. Surely you wouldn't mind if I stole a little peek." He thumbed at the corner of his blindfold.

She admonished him, laughing. "Oh no you don't! If you remove that blindfold, I'll have to turn this car around, mister. You'll have time to look at me later."

"Well, if that's a promise, I'll behave."

After twenty minutes of playful banter, she pulled the car off the road to a small space with barely enough room for two vehicles.

Charlotte got out and went over to his side of the car and opened the door. "Okay, you can remove the blindfold now."

He pulled it off and looked around. "Where are we?" He pushed the door closed and walked a few paces, then looked back at her. "We can't be that far from Candle Beach, because we weren't in the car for very long, but I don't recognize this place."

"That's because not many people know about it." She removed a picnic basket and a beach blanket from the trunk, then grabbed for his hand. "C'mon."

He grasped it, but instead of allowing her to lead him away, he pulled her close and kissed her gently. She stood on her tiptoes and kissed him back, a feeling of exhilaration running through her.

The weather was as perfect as it could get on the Fourth

of July on the Washington Coast, sunny and in the high seventies. They were at her favorite beach, one that she had wanted to take him to since their first date hiking on the trail overlooking the beach. With any luck, this date wouldn't involve an urgent care clinic.

She broke away from him, laughing.

"How did you find this place?" he said as he followed her to the trailhead marker which was almost obscured by the trees.

"I was running on the beach one day, and I saw people coming from somewhere along the cliff. I wasn't familiar with the trail, so I followed them back up to the road." She shrugged. "I've been coming to this spot ever since. It's not usually very busy at this beach, so I like coming here when I need to think."

He took the picnic basket from her and they picked their way down the steep trail to the beach below. She was stepping carefully to avoid jarring her ankle and she noticed his look of concern. "It's okay. My ankle feels fine. I'm just being cautious with it." He nodded and his expression eased.

At dusk, there weren't many people hanging out on the beach. She led him over to a log on the sand and they set up the picnic blanket.

"Will we be able to see the fireworks from Candle Beach here?" Luke opened the picnic basket and pulled out the food, setting it on the blanket.

She nodded. "We should be able to."

They sat on the beach, eating the charcuterie tray that she'd prepared, drinking wine, and talking. She felt as comfortable with him as if she had known him her whole life, and in truth she had. Now, however, there was something more between them.

The sun may have gone down already, but there was still plenty of color in the sky. Luke popped a piece of salami in his mouth and remarked, "It reminds me of one of your paintings, you know—all those colors blending together."

"Hmm," she murmured, resting her head on his shoulder and swirling the wine around in her glass. "I've always enjoyed painting the sky most of all because of that. So many different colors come into play with each other, both at morning and at night. It's almost as if every color you could imagine belonged in there somewhere. It's always fired my imagination."

He reached a hand up to stroke her hair. "I think I envy that about you a bit. You have such a depth of imagination and a passion for creating something beautiful. I'm glad to have gotten to know you better. I didn't see this side of you before."

Lifting her head off his shoulder, she gazed intently at him. She noticed a glint in his eyes from the reflection of the beauty of the scene he was taking in. "I think that both of us didn't see each other for who we truly were at first. Thanks for not giving up too easily." She leaned in and nuzzled at his cheek before kissing it lightly. She let out a contented sigh as he put his arm around her shoulder, pulling her close as she settled her head into the hollow at the base of his neck. She closed her eyes, just relishing being held like this for a while.

As it grew dark, they packed everything back away in the picnic basket so that it would be easy to find in the dark after the fireworks. He sat on the soft dry sand and rested his back against a knobby beach log. She positioned herself between his legs and laid her back against his chest, wrapping his arms around her to warm herself. He didn't provide any objection. Even with the thick sweatshirts they wore, it was getting chilly as the sun went down.

When it was sufficiently dark, pops of color shot up into the air from the direction of Candle Beach, spinning like the insides of a kaleidoscope in the sky before dissipating into the night.

"It's so beautiful," Charlotte sighed. "I've always loved the Fourth of July, ever since I was a little kid. There's something that's always appealed to me about the magic of lights dancing in the sky." She laughed. "Maybe it's the painter in me, seeing art everywhere."

"Was the fourth a big holiday in your family?" he asked as he ran his fingers lazily up and down her sweatshirt-covered arm.

"Yeah, probably one of the biggest. My parents love fireworks too and they have a big party every year. Actually, this is the first year I've ever missed the party."

He stopped what he was doing. "We could have gone. You should have said something."

He sounded alarmed and she turned around to look at him. "Oh, don't worry. I didn't want to go this year. Things haven't been so great between my parents and me lately, and I've always wanted to come down here at night."

"Are you sure? We could still pack up and head down to Haven Shores. If we hurry, we could maybe catch the fireworks there. They usually do them a little later in the evening."

She didn't answer right away, not sure how to explain that she really didn't want to be around her family just then. She stared up at the light show, which was particularly amazing against the backdrop of the inky blue waves. "It's okay, really. I'd rather stay here with you. I knew this would be the perfect place to watch the fireworks. It's so beautiful."

He sighed, then brushed a strand of hair away from her face, caressing her cheek with the backs of his curled fingers. "Yes, beautiful."

She shivered and gazed up at him, before turning her head sideways to see him better. "Thank you for being here with me tonight."

~

Luke's heart leapt. She was thanking him? He was the lucky one to get to spend time with this wonderful woman, who could be as happy and light as a fairy one moment, but serious and honest the next.

He craned his head to the side while turning hers to fully face him with a finger to her chin.

"Thank you for giving me a chance." He cupped her face with one hand and she looked at him in wonder before he lightly brushed his lips against hers. She moved her hands across his chest and up around his neck, lithely rolling to the side onto her hip as she did, so that her upper body pressed squarely against him. Amazingly she never broke the kiss as she moved. Now that she was better positioned, she tightened her embrace while kissing back more deeply. His heart beat faster.

How had he not seen Charlotte as anything other than his best friend's kid sister before this year? How could he have missed this? Now, all he could see was the beautiful, vibrant woman in front of him and he intended to make up for lost time.

He placed his hands on her waist, his fingers touching smooth bare skin where her sweatshirt lifted as she had stretched to wrap her arms around his neck. He gently massaged circles on the small of her back and she broke their kiss to sigh in pleasure, pressing more tightly against him, but not breaking their connection.

She closed her eyes, but he kept his open, not wanting to miss a second. Behind her, the fireworks came to a grand finale, with multiple bursts of color in the air at the same time. She kissed him lightly again and snuggled against his chest to watch. He rested his chin on her head, inhaling the clean floral scent of her shampoo. Everything about her was enchanting.

When the show was over, small beams of light appeared from flashlights as a few other people who had been hidden in the dark readied themselves for the trek back up the trail.

"Should we go?" he whispered to Charlotte.

"Do we have to?" she whispered back. Then she shivered as a blast of cold wind hit them.

"I think we'd better." As much as he'd like nothing more than to stay on the beach with her all night, he could tell she was freezing. He eased her to an upright seated position and stood, holding out his hand to help her to her feet.

"Oh, fine." She took his hand, pulled herself up, and looked into his eyes, her face glowing in the moonlight. "This was so much better than any party at my parents' house."

He pulled her close, dipping her slightly but rapidly, for one last kiss on the beach. "I completely agree."

She let out a muted squeal, startled by the sudden dip, but he could feel the corners of her lips pulled into a smile as he kissed her.

Raising her back up, he slowly released his embrace. He stooped down to retrieve the picnic basket, looping the handle over his arm, and then reached his hand out for hers. "Ready?"

She switched on the flashlight, a warm smile still affixed to her face. "I suppose."

They made their way back up the hill slowly, following the path illuminated by the wavering light of their flashlight.

When they reached the top, she unlocked the car and they stashed the picnic basket and blanket away, then got in.

As she drove, he kept sneaking glances at her. His nerves tingled, remembering how she'd felt in his arms. He wanted to feel that way for the rest of his life. Although it had only been a couple of weeks, he couldn't imagine a future without the woman sitting by his side. Too soon though, they were back in Candle Beach and she was dropping him off at his apartment.

"I'll call you tomorrow morning, before you leave for Seattle, okay?" he said.

She nodded. "I wish you were coming to the show."

"Me too." He felt awful about not being able to attend. A close friend of his was getting married in Texas and he was a groomsman. He'd considered canceling in order to attend Charlotte's show, but she'd talked him out of it, saying that he'd made a commitment to his friend.

He turned to her and kissed her deeply. "Until we see each other again."

She pressed her fingers to her lips and nodded. "In a few days."

He hopped out of the car and waved to her before entering his apartment. It was going to kill him to be parted from her for his long weekend trip away. He'd grown used to seeing her every day at work and spending time with her in the evenings.

It was funny how you never knew what you were

missing until you had it, and then you couldn't imagine anything different. He'd thought Parker was crazy when he said how wonderful it was to work with Gretchen every day, but now he understood.

15

*C*harlotte placed the last item in the overnight bag she'd set on her bed, her stomach alive with butter-flies. Today was it, her solo show at the art gallery in Seattle. This could be one of the most important nights of her life. From the living room came the peals of her cell phone. She jogged over to it and answered without looking at it.

"Hello?"

"Hey," Luke said. The sound of his voice sent shivers of happiness throughout her body, momentarily quelling her anxiety.

"Hey, yourself." She sat down on the couch, bringing her knees up to her chest.

"I wanted to call and tell you to break a leg or whatever it is that people are supposed to wish someone when they have their own showing at a gallery." He paused. "On second thought, I don't think you need a broken leg in addition to the sprained ankle."

She laughed. "I think good luck would be appropriate."

"How's the ankle feeling after hiking up that trail to the beach last night?"

"Actually, not too bad." It may have been a little much to take on so soon after her injury, but the doctor had been right when he'd said it would hurt for a week or two and then start to be less noticeable. Besides, spending last night with Luke in such a perfect location had been completely worth any discomfort she had that morning.

"Anyway, I wanted to wish you good luck then. I'm sorry I can't be there for your show."

"Me too." She looked out the window. Maggie and Gretchen were riding down with her, for which she was grateful, but it wasn't quite the same as having Luke attend.

He sighed. "I could still call Denny and tell him I'm not able to fly out to Houston for his wedding."

"Don't be silly," she said with as much enthusiasm as she could muster. "You're a groomsman. You can't cancel out on him at the last minute."

"I know. But it doesn't seem right to miss your show. I'd love to be there and see everyone excited about your work."

His enthusiasm over her art made her blush, but felt amazing. Having someone so supportive about her dreams was something she never thought she'd have.

"It's okay. Don't even worry about it. We're going to have a girls' night out and will have a ton of fun."

"I hope you do. And take a bunch of pictures too. I want to see all of your adoring fans."

She laughed. "I'm not sure that's appropriate in a fancy art gallery, but I'll see what I can do. You may just get pictures of us hanging out afterward."

"I'll take what I can get." He sighed. "I'd better let you go. Bye, Charlotte. Good luck."

"Bye, Luke. Don't have too much fun at the bachelor party."

He laughed. "I don't think you'll have to worry too much.

Denny is a pretty conservative guy. I'm not sure what's in store for us, but it probably doesn't involve anything you'd be concerned about." His voice softened. "I love you."

His words left her speechless. Before she could think of how to respond, he hung up. Luke had just told her he loved her. Tears came to her eyes and she didn't think her heart could get any fuller. Part of her wanted to call him back and tell him she loved him too, but for some reason, she hung back. Although she felt what they had was real, a small part of her was hanging on to disbelief that someone like him could really love her.

~

A knock sounded on the hotel room door.

"Hello?" she called out.

"Flower delivery for Ms. Gray," a man answered.

Gretchen was closest to the door of their hotel room. "I'll get it."

She peered through the peephole, then opened the door to reveal a man carrying a huge bouquet of red roses. He thrust them at her and spun around quickly, apparently eager to get to his next delivery.

Gretchen shut the door and carried the roses to Charlotte. "They're beautiful. Are they from Luke?"

Charlotte's heart skipped a few beats. She hadn't told her friends about his declaration of love because she still wasn't quite sure how she felt about it and she didn't want to be barraged with well-meaning questions. She took the flowers from Gretchen and retrieved the card from the base of the bouquet. Unexpectedly, she felt a sense of loss. "Nope, they're from my parents."

Congrats, honey. Sorry we couldn't make it. Love, Mom

and Dad.

The words were friendly, but the reminder that they weren't attending such a big event in her life stung.

"That was nice of them." Maggie's eyes were trained on Charlotte's face, assessing her reaction.

"Yeah."

"But it would have been better if they were here, right?" Gretchen said. "I'm not sure if I should say this because they're my future in-laws, but it wouldn't kill them to take more of an interest in their children as people."

Charlotte felt a rush of love for her future sister-in-law. She reached out and hugged her. "I'm glad you're going to be part of my family. Parker needs someone like you."

Gretchen blushed. "Thanks." She glanced at the other two women. "Are you ready to go?"

Charlotte smoothed the pleats of the black cocktail dress she'd borrowed from Dahlia. "I think so."

"Then let's go," Maggie said warmly. "I can't wait to see your paintings hanging in an art gallery."

They walked over to the gallery and entered the main room. Although she'd just been there a few days prior in the daylight, the gallery was transformed at night. And her paintings. Those were *her* paintings hanging on the wall. Tears pooled in the corners of her eyes. It all seemed surreal.

Gretchen grabbed her hand and squeezed it, then pulled her over to one of the artworks. "I love this sunset painting. It's similar to the one in my living room that you gave me."

Charlotte nodded. "Sunsets are my favorite because they're so alive and change from minute to minute. It's a challenge to get them just right."

"They're fantastic," Maggie said, giving her a quick hug. "I think the other people like them too." She nudged Charlotte around to see two couples pointing at her painting of Bluebonnet Lake and discussing it animatedly.

She sucked in her breath and spun around slowly. These were all hers. She'd been given the chance at a solo show and now her work had to stand on its own. With any luck, people would respond well to it.

"Charlotte," Raymond said, coming up to her. "I'd like for you to meet some people." She followed him to a corner of the gallery and the evening became a whirlwind of new people to meet. He told her that he'd give her a call in the next day or so to let her know how many paintings she'd sold.

Gretchen and Maggie had returned to their room an hour earlier, so when the gallery closed for the night, Charlotte walked back to the hotel alone.

They mobbed her when she entered the room.

"Congratulations," Maggie said as she hugged her.

"People loved it!" Gretchen exclaimed.

Her heart swelled with happiness. "Thank you, you guys. I really appreciate you coming tonight." Then she looked around the room. "What are we going to do now? We're three semi-single women out for a night in the big city. It's only ten o'clock. We should go out or something."

"With my wedding coming up soon, it's almost like we're having a bachelorette party." Maggie laughed. "But unlike the one I had before my first wedding, this one is going to be tamer. It's too bad Dahlia and Angel weren't able to come tonight."

Gretchen smiled. "I remember your bachelorette party. I thought you were going to have a panic attack when that man entered dressed as a police officer and started taking off his clothes." She shook her head. "I don't know what Kari was thinking when she hired him."

Maggie grimaced. "I remember. I thought Brian's eyes were going to bug out of his head when I told him about having to ask the guy to leave." Her eyes misted over. "He thought it was hilarious."

Charlotte wasn't sure what to say, so she just patted Maggie's arm. "It's pretty late already. I think the craziest thing we'll be doing tonight might be hitting up the Cheesecake Factory for a late-night dessert."

"Ooh." Gretchen's eyes lit up. "That sounds good. I could go for something sweet. They make the best turtle cheesecake there."

Maggie checked her watch. "If we hurry, we can make it down the street before they close."

They giggled like little girls as they changed out of the cocktail attire they'd worn to the gallery and walked out of the hotel into the warm evening. It was one of those rare nights where there wasn't much of a breeze and the air was almost muggy, trapping all of the odors of city life at street level.

Charlotte wrinkled her nose as they passed an alley. "Eww."

Gretchen nodded. "Makes you glad to live in a small town, huh?"

"No kidding." Maggie pushed open the door to the Cheesecake Factory and they were blasted with fresh, cold air.

The host greeted the three of them and led them to a small booth in the corner of the restaurant. "Your server will be with you momentarily." He placed menus on the table and left.

"It's been a while since I've been here." Charlotte scanned the menu. "I'm actually hungry. When we had dinner before the show, I couldn't eat because my stomach was flip-flopping too much. I think I'll get the Thai Lettuce Wraps now."

"Not me," Gretchen said. "I'm getting the turtle cheesecake." She closed the menu and pushed it to the edge of the table. "So how are you feeling? I thought people seemed like they were enjoying your work."

"I know I did." Maggie sipped from the glass of ice water the waiter had placed in front of her. "I really loved that painting of the sun setting behind the candlestick."

"Thanks." Charlotte beamed. "It's my favorite too. I'll actually be sad to let it go when someone buys it. Part of me wants to keep it for myself." She'd begun painting it one night after setting her easel up at a beach overlook high above the candlestick-shaped rock that gave Candle Beach its name. "Luke really likes it too."

"Ah, Luke." Gretchen gave her a knowing look. "I bet he was upset that he couldn't be there with you tonight. He seems quite devoted."

"Yeah." Charlotte stared out the window at the sidewalks, still bustling with people leaving the theater or coming from a late dinner at one of the many restaurants downtown. "He felt bad about it, but he had to go to that wedding."

"So, is he going to be your date for my wedding?" Maggie asked.

The waiter came back and took their orders, giving Charlotte a moment to think. She and Luke had been dating for a couple of weeks, but she hadn't asked him yet about coming with her to Maggie and Jake's wedding.

"I'm not sure." She wrapped her hand around her water

glass, her fingers clearing spots on the surface condensation. "Probably."

"Good." Maggie smiled. "We like him."

"You do?" Charlotte cocked her head to the side. "I didn't think you knew him very well."

"We met when he came to the Sorensen Farm to make arrangements for parking his food truck there for catering the Bike Barn fundraiser."

"Ah." That made sense. She'd forgotten about that.

"Parker doesn't want to ask you himself, but he'd like to know how things are going between you and Luke," Gretchen announced.

Charlotte blushed. Her brother had always been nosy regarding her love life, but at least he was interested in her life. She couldn't say the same for her parents.

"Tell him that it's a private matter."

"I have to tell him something!" Gretchen said. "C'mon. Do you see this as a long-term thing?"

She sighed. "Yes." It suddenly flooded over her that she did see a future for herself and Luke. "Before he left, he told me that he loved me."

"He did?" Maggie said, wide-eyed. "What did you say?"

"I didn't have a chance to say anything." Now, however, she was certain that she felt the same way. Having him not here to share in her special night had made her realize how important he'd become to her. "I think I feel the same way about him," she admitted.

"But?" Maggie asked. "You don't seem completely sure."

"But I'm still worried about his money. You know how my family is—I don't want to fall into that trap again. I've worked hard for what I have."

Gretchen nodded. "Parker is the same with money.

Everything we do with the company is five times more difficult than it needs to be because he doesn't want to be seen as leaning on his parents in the slightest." She gave Charlotte a hard look. "But Luke isn't the same as your parents. I've never seen anything but kindness from him, and you'd never guess he had gobs of money."

Charlotte laughed. "I don't think he wants people to know. He didn't grow up with money, so I worry it could become a problem in the future as he starts to take it for granted."

The waiter came by with their food and Gretchen dug into her cheesecake.

"But he's never given you any reason to think that, right?" Maggie asked before taking a bite of her cheesecake which was overflowing with blueberries.

"No," Charlotte sighed. "Not really." He wasn't overly concerned about how much he spent on things, but he wasn't terribly frivolous either. "I guess I'm being silly."

"I agree," Gretchen said. "But I do understand your concerns."

"Still, you shouldn't borrow trouble. If there isn't a problem now, don't make it into one," Maggie said. "Or talk to him about how you feel. Maybe he can assuage some of your fears."

Charlotte considered Maggie's advice. She knew she should admit to Luke how she felt about his money, so why was it so difficult to actually do so?

"Yeah. Communication is always good," Gretchen said. "Believe me. If you're not honest about things, they have a way of building up and spilling out, which causes even more problems."

"I guess. It's just hard to talk to him about such things.

Not that I don't trust him to listen, but in my family, we never communicated much. I'm probably bad at it." Charlotte spooned some filling into a piece of butter lettuce. When she bit into it, the lettuce made a satisfying crunch and gave the seasoned filling a burst of moisture.

"Pshaw." Maggie held out her fork. "Just tell him how you feel. He's a good guy, he'll understand."

Charlotte finished eating her lettuce wrap but didn't say anything. It was easy to talk about communicating with someone else, but reality was something completely different.

Gretchen seemed to notice how uncomfortable Charlotte was and changed the subject. "How are the wedding plans going, Maggie?"

Charlotte breathed a sigh of relief that the well-meaning advice session seemed to be over.

Maggie's face lit up. "Great! It's amazing how much easier it is to plan a small wedding than a large one. With my first wedding, I would lie awake and stare at the ceiling at night, wondering if I'd remembered everything. With it just being close friends and family at this one, I figure if I've forgotten something, they'll understand." She laughed. "Plus, it helps that I own the venue."

"It'll be a beautiful wedding," Charlotte said. "I can't wait to see what the barn looks like for the fundraiser and your wedding."

"Yeah, no kidding," Gretchen added. "It's so different than when you first bought it." She wrinkled her nose. "I mean, I could see the potential, but it was no place for an event when I first showed you the property."

"Jake thought the same thing about the barn. But wonderful things can come out of rough beginnings."

Maggie scraped the last bite of creamy cheesecake and blueberry syrup off of her plate.

Charlotte stirred her fork through some of the chicken and vegetables that had fallen out of her wraps. Her relationship with Luke had certainly come from a beginning that was less than smooth, but she was optimistic about their future together.

16

The next morning, Charlotte awoke to sun streaming through the gap that always seemed to slip through hotel curtains, no matter how tightly you closed them the night before. The rest of the room was dark and quiet.

She rolled over to see Gretchen still sleeping next to her.

"Good morning," Maggie whispered from where she was sitting at the desk with a cup of coffee in her hands and her laptop open in front of her.

"Coffee?" Charlotte motioned blearily to the coffee pot. She was useless before her first cup of the day.

Maggie laughed quietly. "I'll get you a cup." She walked over to the single-cup coffee maker and set it up to brew.

Charlotte picked up her clothes, then padded to the bathroom in her pajamas. After getting dressed, she splashed some water on her face and stared at herself in the mirror. Dark circles had appeared under her eyes from stress and not enough sleep in the weeks leading up to the art show, but the way she felt was completely opposite. After the successful show the night before, she could take on anything.

Maggie set a steaming hot cup of coffee on the counter in front of her. She blew on the liquid at the top and took a cautious sip. Ahh. Caffeine.

Gretchen sat up in bed, her dark hair tangled around her shoulders. "Am I the last one to wake up?"

"Yes, sleepyhead," Maggie teased. "And we'd better get going. It's almost nine and I want to make sure we're home well before the dinner rush."

"Yes, Mother," Gretchen said, favoring Maggie with a mock-glare. She jumped out of bed and grabbed her clothes out of her bag. "Do we have time for breakfast at the hotel coffee shop?"

Maggie nodded. "If we hurry."

Maggie and Gretchen finish packing their suitcases first and lined them up by the door. Charlotte was almost done packing hers when the phone rang.

She looked to see who was calling. Raymond from the art gallery. She held out the keys to Gretchen.

"I have to take this call, but here are the keys so you can put your stuff in the car. I'll meet you downstairs at the coffee shop when I'm done."

As they left, Charlotte hurriedly pressed the button on her phone to accept the call.

"Hi, Raymond."

"Charlotte. I wanted to touch base with you about the show last night." He cleared his throat.

"Okay." What did he want to talk with her about? She'd felt pretty good about last night. Maybe she'd sold all her paintings. A thrill shot through her.

"About the show. We didn't sell as many paintings as we hoped for."

Her heart sank. "How many were sold?" She hoped at least a few, although she wouldn't be too upset if the one of the sun setting over the candlestick rock wasn't one of them.

He cleared his throat again. "None of them yet."

She froze near the hotel room door with her hand on her suitcase. "None of them?"

"This sometimes happens with new artists. I'll ship anything back to you that doesn't sell in the next couple of days in the gallery."

"Oh. Well, thank you. I appreciate you taking a chance on me."

"You're very welcome. It was nice to meet you Charlotte, and I enjoyed working with you."

He hung up and she couldn't do anything but stare at the wall. How was it that she'd been so happy only a minute before and now she felt as though her world was crashing down upon her? All she wanted to do was call Luke. Luke. She had somebody to call, somebody she could count on to share in her news, good or bad.

She quickly dialed him, but the phone rang and rang. When she got his voicemail, she hung up, then reconsidered. Maybe he hadn't heard it ringing. She tried again. The same thing. This time, she left a message. Hopefully he'd get back to her soon. She gave the hotel room a once-over and determined that they hadn't left anything behind. Then she dragged her suitcase down the hall, the wheels leaving behind a trail of crushed carpet before she entered the elevator. When the elevator stopped in the lobby, she found Gretchen and Maggie waiting for her. They still had their suitcases with them.

"You're still here," she said in surprise. "I told you that you could go put your stuff in the car." They'd parked her car in the parking lot near the hotel to avoid paying for valet parking.

"Eh. We figured we would just wait for you," Maggie said. "It seemed easier than us going separately and then having to try to find you afterward."

"Okay, thanks." Charlotte's eyes blurred with tears.

"What's wrong?" Maggie asked sharply, immediately going into mom mode.

Gretchen looked at her more closely. "Who was that on the phone?"

Charlotte bit her lip. "It was the gallery owner." She didn't want to admit to them that her show had been a dismal failure.

"I take it that it wasn't good news." Gretchen moved away from her suitcase and came over to Charlotte, wrapping her arm around her.

"No." Charlotte fought to keep from crying.

Maggie came over too. "I'm sorry, Charlotte. I'm sure it will all turn out okay."

She just nodded. If she said anything, her words would probably turn to sobs. Instead, she let herself be comforted by her two friends. Her friends that had come all the way from Candle Beach to see her art show, and believed in her and her work. She should be happy that she could count on them, so why did she find herself wishing that her parents and Luke were there too?

"Well, let's get these suitcases out to the car and get some more coffee into us." Maggie reached for her suitcase and led them out of the hotel and to the car.

"And plenty of pancakes," Gretchen said. "I think we could all use a sugar and carbohydrate coma."

"Thanks, guys." Charlotte smiled gratefully at her friends. If they hadn't been there, she didn't know what she'd have done. Driving home knowing that people hadn't liked her art would be painful, but she knew they'd do their best to distract her.

~

When Charlotte returned to her shop after dropping Maggie off at the café and Gretchen at her house, Sandra, the teenager she'd hired to help out over the summer jogged up to her, carrying a sheet of paper.

"Is something wrong?" Charlotte asked.

"Some old guy dropped off an eviction notice." She held out the paper, her arm wavering as her eyes met Charlotte's.

"What?" Charlotte grabbed it from her and quickly scanned the document. Sure enough, it read EVICTION in big capital letters. "I have to move out within three days?"

Sandra shrugged and her tank top rose above her waistband. She tugged it back down. "He said to tell you he's tried to contact you through the mail, but you haven't responded."

Charlotte's mind flashed back to the stack of mail still sitting on an end table in her living room. She'd been meaning to open it, but had been so busy that it had piled up and may have been there longer than she'd intended.

"Thanks." Her voice was tight, then warmed slightly as she addressed her employee. "I appreciate you working today. It's such a nice day—I'm sure you'd have rather been out with your friends or something."

Sandra shrugged again. "I don't mind. I need to earn money for college next fall. Let me know if you need my help again. Oh, and it was a little slow, so I organized the inventory under the counters."

Charlotte nodded. "Thank you."

Sandra left and she walked inside the trailer and sat down at her stool behind the cash register. Everything looked in order, right down to the neatly filed receipts in the folder next to the register. How was it that a seventeen-year-old seemed to have better organizational skills than Charlotte did in her late twenties?

She picked up the eviction notice again. Why was her landlord kicking her out? There had to be some mistake.

She checked the time. Two o'clock. If she closed the shop, she could probably make it over to the landlord's office and back in thirty minutes. Then she could get this mess sorted out.

After locking up Whimsical Delights, she walked the few blocks over to her landlord's house, where he maintained an office with an exterior entrance in a converted garage. A car was parked in the carport of the neatly painted green house.

She knocked on the office door, which was open slightly to take advantage of the breeze.

"Come in," he said, without looking up.

"Hi, Mr. Devine."

He looked up, his white hair fuzzing around his head like a puffy cloud. "Ms. Gray." He lowered his reading glasses. "Did you get the notice I dropped off at your trailer? You weren't there, but I gave it to someone I assume is your employee."

"I did get it. That's actually why I'm here." She sat down in the chair across from him. "I'd intended to extend my lease for another year. How can I make that happen?"

He pressed his lips together. "I'm sorry, but I've already leased the space you were occupying. I contacted you about a renewal, but I didn't receive a response so I figured you didn't want to renew it."

Her eyes widened and she leaned forward, causing the hard, plastic seat to dig into her thighs. She knew not taking the time to open her mail would come back to bite her. "I'm sorry. Isn't there anything I can do?"

He shook his head. "No. Your lease was up a month ago, and the new tenant signed for the space a while ago."

"Can you at least tell me who is taking the space? Maybe I can talk with them." She peered at him. "I love the location I'm in right now and I don't want to have to move."

He sighed. "I suppose it wouldn't hurt to tell you. Luke Tisdale with that barbecue food truck is taking over the whole space. He said something about wanting room for more picnic tables. I didn't catch all of the details."

She leaned back, her mind spinning. Luke was the reason she was losing her space? How was that possible? He wouldn't do that to her. He'd just told her that he loved her. This was nuts.

"Are you sure? Can you please check your records?" She held her breath, hoping that Mr. Devine had remembered incorrectly.

"Of course, I'm sure." He glanced at his computer and then back to her, before shuffling some papers around on his desk. "Look, I've got work to do. I'd have been happy to rent to you for the coming year if you'd answered the letters that I sent you, but the truth remains—you didn't respond. I'm a businessman and I can't wait for people to get around to talking to me."

She bit her lip. "It wasn't like that." She stopped. Somehow, telling him that she hadn't bothered to open the mail he'd sent her didn't seem like a smart move either. If only he'd called or something, but he was very old-school and that wasn't how he ran his business. She stood. "I'll talk to

Luke about it. If I can get him to back out of taking over my spot, will you let me rent the space?"

He waved in the air. "Fine. Let me know what he decides."

She left the office feeling both better and worse than when she'd entered. There was a chance that she could get her space back if she could convince Luke to relinquish it. But there was still the question of why he'd done it in the first place. She'd thought they had something special between them and now he'd stabbed her in the back. Was this why he wasn't answering her calls? Was he too embarrassed to admit that he'd stolen her spot?

She made her way back to the trailer on autopilot, seeing the Airstream parked there that she'd worked so hard to purchase. She'd gritted her teeth and worked for her parents for years to earn enough money to purchase it outright and buy inventory for the store. The trailer was beautiful, exactly what she'd wanted for her shop.

If she couldn't renew her lease, how was she going to operate her business? Empty lots in areas of Candle Beach with high tourist traffic were few and far between. She'd made a lot of friends in this town and she hoped it wouldn't come down to moving her business elsewhere.

17

*L*uke couldn't wait to get back to Candle Beach, but his plane was delayed by several hours and by the time he arrived in town, it was after eleven at night. He showered and fell into bed, exhausted.

The long weekend had been too full. When he got to Houston, his friend had whisked him and the other groomsmen away to a camping trip in a remote area for two days, and then back to the hotel just in time for the wedding. He'd wanted to call Charlotte, but there hadn't been cell service or electricity where they'd camped, and then his phone had been dead the day of the ceremony. He missed seeing her or hearing her voice at the very least.

Early the next morning when he went to the food truck to start up the smoker, he found a note taped to the door.

Luke—we need to talk. Charlotte

What was that all about? He'd intended to check in with her as soon as he got back, but his plane had been late and he hadn't wanted to bother her so late at night. He checked his watch. Six a.m. He glanced at the Airstream trailer. He'd wait and talk to her in person when she got in to work.

Not knowing about why Charlotte wanted to talk to him was killing him. In his experience, when a woman said they needed to talk, it was usually to break up with him. As far as he knew, everything was great between the two of them, but then again, when he'd told her he loved her, she'd said nothing. He'd thought it was because the timing was wrong or that he hadn't given her a chance to respond and they hadn't talked since, but what if that wasn't true?

She knocked on his door a few hours later while he was chopping sweet potatoes into fries.

"Hey," he said, smiling at her. "How was the show? I really wish I could have been there." He set down the knife and removed his gloves, then stepped toward her, stopping when she frowned at him.

"Hi." She took a deep breath. "Why did you take over the lease on my half of the lot?"

Her words reverberated through his brain. What was she talking about?

"What?"

"Mr. Devine told me he isn't renewing my lease. Said you'd already signed for the other half of the lot."

Ice shot through his veins. He vaguely remembered that amid everything else he'd done in preparation for opening a business in Candle Beach, the landlord had asked him if he'd be interested in expanding to the rest of the site after a few months. He'd said yes, not knowing that the other tenant was Charlotte.

"Oh." How was he going to explain this to her?

"Oh?" She cocked her head to the side. "So, you did sign for my half of the property?" Her voice escalated in volume with each word.

"No. Well, yes." He shook his head. "I did sign the lease, but I had no idea at the time that you were leasing the other half of the lot. And Mr. Devine told me that you wouldn't be there much longer—I do remember that. I was in the middle of getting a business license, arranging to move the truck here, and figuring out how to advertise the food truck, and I totally forgot I'd signed the lease for the extra space." He peered at her. "Did you tell him you didn't want the space? It seems odd he offered it to me without talking to you first."

She averted her eyes. "There was a mix-up, but I had no intention of leaving. I love it here." She motioned to the lot. "Do you need all of it?"

"No, of course not. Our current arrangement is fine. I can fix this. Do you think he'd let me sublease it to you?"

She sighed in relief. "He said if you agreed, it was fine with him."

He felt a smile spread across his face. "Great."

"Great." She smiled back at him. "So how much do I owe you for my half?"

He held up a finger. "Let me check my paperwork." He disappeared into the truck, then reappeared holding the lease he hadn't looked at in several months. "So, half would be ..." He gave her the amount.

Her jaw dropped. "That's twice what I was paying before. I can't afford that." Tears appeared in the corners of her eyes.

His stomach lurched. He had no idea that she was paying less than him. If he had, he would have told her a lesser amount. "Uh, maybe I figured that wrong. Yeah, it should be half of that for your half."

Her eyes narrowed in suspicion. "What's the total? You're telling me less because you don't think I can afford it, right?"

He couldn't do anything but stare at her. Every second felt like a minute as he tried to figure out what to say that would fix the situation. He didn't need the extra space and subsidizing her rent was no big deal in his budget. All he wanted was for Charlotte to stay there and be happy.

"That's it, isn't it?" The tears started to fall. "I can't accept charity from you."

"Charlotte, wait. It's not charity." His words fell upon deaf ears as she whirled around and ran into her trailer.

He didn't know whether or not to follow her but opted to give her a little space. An hour later, he approached the trailer. She called out a greeting, obviously thinking he was a potential customer, but her spine stiffened when she realized it was him.

"What do you want?" she asked.

He stopped in front of the trailer. "I want to talk about the lease. You have to believe me. I had no idea that it was you renting the space or that you actually wanted to stay. I only went along with what Mr. Devine told me."

She balled up her fists, then uncurled them and lay them flat in front of her on the counter.

"It doesn't really matter. I can't afford to sublease from you. I'll have to look for a new space." Her voice was dull, a stark contrast to the joy she usually exhibited.

He felt as though he'd been punched in the gut. Was she really this stubborn? He could afford the extra cost.

"Really, I can help you. It's no big deal."

She stared at him in horror. "No big deal to pay for half of my rent? Are you serious? Do you know me at all?"

This was getting worse by the minute. "I just wanted to help you."

Her jaw tightened. "I don't need your help. Goodbye." She stood and grabbed the handle to the trailer door, slamming it shut in his face.

He stood there, shocked. What had just happened?

When she showed no sign of opening the door again, he

reluctantly went back to the food truck to finish prepping for lunch. Throughout the day, he surreptitiously checked what she was doing, but she made no attempt to contact him. After the dinner crowd, he shut down the truck and made his way over to her trailer, where she was totaling the day's receipts.

When she saw him, she stopped what she was doing.

"Luke." She bit her lip.

"I'm so sorry. I didn't mean to take the lease. Or offend you, or whatever. Just let me make it up to you."

She regarded him sadly. "I don't think this is going to work out."

Terror filled his chest, sucking out any air. "What do you mean?"

"I can't be with someone that doesn't think I can make it on my own. I'm having enough trouble making myself believe that at the moment. I think I need to be alone for a while."

He took a deep breath, fighting to stay calm. "Can I change your mind?"

"No," she whispered. "Goodbye, Luke." She stepped out of the trailer and locked the door, then brushed past him and disappeared around the block.

His mind buzzed. He'd gone from excitement the night before about seeing her again to disbelief that they were over today. He'd thought he'd finally met the woman he'd been looking for his entire life. How had this gone so wrong so quickly?

~

"So, what do you think?" Gretchen motioned to the abandoned lot she'd just shown Charlotte as a possibility for parking her trailer.

The empty lot was bordered by a rickety fence that hadn't seen a coat of paint in many years. Dust flew through the air with each step they took in the dusty dirt and gravel mix that half covered the ground. A neglected rosebush fought for nutrients in an old flowerbed in a corner of the lot near the sidewalk. If she craned her neck up, there was a possible view of the ocean, but otherwise there wasn't much to recommend the place.

"Is this the only available space in town?" Charlotte scanned the space again, grimacing. This couldn't be happening. Maybe if she closed her eyes and reopened them, she'd magically have her space back again—the space she'd inhabited for over a year. Anger rose involuntarily within her. If Luke hadn't showed up in town, this never would have happened. As soon as she thought that, a little voice whispered that if she hadn't been so disorganized this wouldn't have happened. She fought to tamp down the negative thoughts.

Gretchen nodded. "Yeah, sorry. It's the only place that would make sense for a retail business. I think this would be good for you though." She pointed. "See, that building over there will house an art gallery and a small restaurant of some type. We're only a block over from Main Street, so with a nice sign, people will easily find you."

Charlotte stared at the two-story structure being built across the street. Construction workers wearing hard hats were erecting walls while a man holding a clipboard shouted instructions to them. The noise of drills and hammering was deafening.

Her gaze turned toward Main Street. A car drove by and people crossed the street as they headed down the hill, but none came along the sidewalk in their direction. Even if Gretchen was right and the space would eventually receive more retail traffic, it would be miserable and noisy until then—if that traffic ever materialized.

"I guess," she said. "It's not as nice as my old space though."

Her heart ached thinking about what she'd lost—both the lot lease and her relationship with Luke. She still wasn't sure she'd made the right decision to end things with him, but she felt it was something she had to do. Too much time had been spent fighting for financial independence for her to give it up so easily. He'd acted as though it was no big deal to help her with the rent, but he didn't understand how important it was to her to make it on her own. If he couldn't understand that, it wouldn't work between them.

"No," Gretchen agreed. "It's not as nice. But I think you can make it your own. Plus, it's bigger than the old location."

"True. But it's not the same." She surveyed the lot again. Still dusty and empty, but the scent of roses drifted over to them. Maybe it would be better once her trailer was parked there and she could make it more of her own space.

Gretchen smiled gently and squeezed Charlotte's arm. "Is it because you don't like the space, or because it's lacking a certain neighbor?"

"Both maybe." Charlotte sighed. "Okay. I'll take it. I've got to find somewhere to park the trailer and I'll lose money for every day I don't have somewhere to sell to my customers."

"Good. I think you're making the right decision." Gretchen motioned up the hill. "Do you want to come back to the office and sign the paperwork now?"

Charlotte took one last look at the site. "Might as well."

Nothing about this situation was going to be the same.

She'd found part of herself at the old site—learning how to be a successful business owner and making it on her own. Now because of Luke—and her own mistakes—she'd have to start all over again. At least it was in Candle Beach. If she had to leave her friends and established customer base, she didn't know what she'd do.

Finding someone to move her trailer hadn't been easy, but now that they were backing it into her new lot, she could focus on making the dumpy lot better.

"That's far enough," she called out to the truck driver. He nodded and halted the vehicle, then went around to the back and unhitched the trailer.

"You should be good now," he said in a gruff voice.

"Thank you so much." She handed him some cash and he stuffed it in his pocket.

"Good luck, miss." He got back into his truck and drove away.

She adjusted the jacks on either side until the trailer was level, then brushed her hands off on her jeans. Slowly turning in a circle, she surveyed the lot. Unfortunately, it hadn't magically turned into a beautiful garden. She swallowed a lump that had formed in her throat, thinking about how close she and Luke had been at the old lot, both emotionally, and in proximity.

What's done is done. There was no use thinking about how nice her old space had been. She squared her shoulders. Now was the time to make this space her own. The old spot hadn't been nearly as nice when she'd first moved in, and she'd transformed it. She could do the same now.

Charlotte grabbed a notebook from the trailer and listed

out the things that she'd need to do—buy oyster shells for a pathway, some more plants, maybe a bench or two. She grew excited thinking about the possibilities. The lot was bigger than the old shared one, and with the sunlight here, she could grow flowers in a garden.

She eyed the construction across the street. That was harder to put a rosy picture on, but there wasn't anything she could do about it. She'd have to make some more signs. Being a block off Main Street was a challenge, but when had she ever backed away from a challenge?

With a stick, she drew a pathway from the sidewalk to her trailer. With a border of stones and a crushed oyster shell path, it would do nicely. A familiar figure stood on Main Street, looking toward her trailer. What was Luke doing there?

She turned away, sneaking peeks at him, but he didn't come any closer and soon left. Her stomach twisted. A couple of weeks ago, everything had been great and now it was all messed up. She missed Luke, and even though she kept reminding herself of why they wouldn't work, she couldn't get rid of the wistfulness that hit her every time she thought of him.

18

*L*uke stirred the vats of shredded smoked pork and placed yet another pan of cornbread in the oven to bake in preparation for the Bike Barn barbecue. With a great deal of satisfaction, he looked around the inside of the food truck. It had been a ton of work, but things were shaping up for the guests' arrival in an hour.

He'd pulled the truck up to the Sorensen Farm an hour earlier and parked it in a grassy area, away from the main event space. For the barbecue, he wouldn't be serving from his truck, but it was still nice to have the cooking facility right there on site. He'd heard Maggie had plans for a catering kitchen, but she hadn't constructed one yet, so it would come in handy.

He stepped out of the stiflingly hot truck and into the meager amount of shade it provided from the warm July sun. Although Maggie hadn't been able to help much in planning, she'd provided picnic tables, serving dishes and silverware for the event. Charlotte was already there when he'd arrived, and from the harried expression on her face, she must have been there for hours. They hadn't spoken since the day she'd broken up with him, but he'd checked on her from a distance while she was at the new lot where she'd set up shop. For a minute, he'd thought she'd seen him, but then she'd turned and looked away, so he left. He'd left a note for Charlotte with Dahlia, begging her to reconsider, but he hadn't heard anything back.

He looked around the event area. He had to admit it, she'd been right about the decorations making or breaking an event. The pieces she'd chosen for this event were definitely on the making it side. She'd covered the tables with cheery red and blue checkered tablecloths and set baskets full of blue flowers on each. A long buffet table held warming dishes and she'd found an antique wooden picnic basket to exhibit the rolls and cornbread muffins. They all combined to make an inviting place for people to hang out and enjoy the evening—and hopefully donate money.

He wandered over to the barn. Charlotte was scurrying around inside, straightening items for the silent auction and checking in with the band that would be playing live country music later that night.

"Do you need any help?" He leaned against the open frame of the double barn doors.

She looked up, startled. "Are you done already? What time is it?"

"Almost five. Everything's ready to put on the buffet as soon as people start to arrive." He took a closer look around the room. "It looks great in here."

"Really? Do you think so?"

"Yes. Everyone will love it." He smiled. "And you were right. The extra decorations really have made a difference."

She peered at him and then a small smile broke out upon her lips. "Thank you."

"Uh, do you need to change your clothes before the

guests arrive?" He pointed at her gray sweatpants and tank top. In his opinion, she looked adorable, but she probably intended to wear something dressier for the event.

She stared down at her clothes in horror. "I got so caught up in everything, I totally forgot."

"Do you have a change of clothes here?"

She nodded. "Yes, they're in the farmhouse. Can you be on point here in case anyone has questions while I'm gone?"

"Of course."

"I'll hurry." She jogged off in the direction of the farmhouse.

He sighed. It seemed like she was thawing toward him, but he didn't know if they'd ever get to the point where she'd want to be friends with him again. He hated the thought of a future without her in it, but he couldn't push any more than he already had.

The guests arrived and Luke stayed busy helping Maggie's catering staff set up the buffet. Around him, everyone was laughing and having a good time. Both of the paddleboats were in use on the lake, and he'd seen quite a few people hovering around the silent auction tables. The fundraiser was a success. Charlotte should be proud of herself. It was too bad Pops hadn't been able to come, but he didn't like driving at night and hadn't wanted to miss out on his weekly poker game anyway. Luke supposed it was probably for the best though, as he hadn't yet told Pops that he and Charlotte had broken up. The old man had fallen in love with her and Luke hadn't found the right time to tell him that they were no longer an item.

Soon, Charlotte made her way to the front of the barn.

"Hello, everyone," she said into the microphone. "It's so exciting to see so many people here to help support Saul. He and the Bike Barn have been an integral part of this community for many years and we all know that he'd do anything to help out anyone in need. It's nice to be able to give back to him." She motioned to the silent auction items. "We'll be ending the silent auction soon and starting dinner, but I wanted to take a moment to thank everyone who came tonight and especially the people and businesses who donated to the auction. We couldn't have done it without you."

At a table near the front, Saul stood. He looked at Charlotte and gestured for the microphone. She handed it to him and he spoke.

"I wanted to thank you all personally from the bottom of my heart. When I came to town after my wife died, I didn't know what to expect, but I've felt welcomed from the very first day." He brushed away a tear from his eye and his voice shook. "Seeing the Bike Barn on fire was one of the worst days of my life and I thought everything I'd built here was gone. But then you all came to my rescue." He lowered the mike for a few seconds and then brought it back to chin level. "Thank you." He handed it back to Charlotte, who smiled at him.

"Thank *you,* Saul, for everything you do for this community." She beamed at the crowd. "Now, let's eat!"

Everyone cheered and moved toward the buffet tables. Luke ran food between the truck and the buffet tables until he felt as though his legs and arms would give out. The attendees loved his food though and their compliments gave him strength to continue.

The dinner portion of the event wound up and he helped with cleanup while the dancing started. As he cleared tables and packed up leftover food, he watched with envy as couples swirled around the dance floor together. Charlotte stood near the band surveying the room. She'd changed into a white strapless sundress with pink flowers on it and had placed a matching pink flower behind her ear. Her blonde hair swung around her shoulders as she walked briskly across the room to address the catering staff.

His heart ached, wishing that he could whisk her off her feet and onto the dance floor—wanting her to be his again. The intensity of the emotion surprised him. How was it possible that a few months ago he'd barely given her a thought and now she was the most important person in the world to him?

He retreated to the food truck to finish cleaning up and to avoid seeing her again. When he reappeared, most of the guests had left. He went into the barn to see if there was anything else he could do and saw Charlotte standing with an older man and woman that he recognized as her and Parker's parents. He started to approach them, to ask if she needed help with anything, but stopped when he heard her mother's tone of voice.

"Honey, that's what we were afraid of. The world of art is tough." Her mother patted her arm condescendingly. "Painting isn't going to get you anywhere. We've been telling you that all your life."

Charlotte turned to the side and he could tell she was close to tears. In a shaky voice, she said, "I love painting."

"But you have to be practical, Charlotte," her father said. "Has your business turned a profit yet?"

She took a deep breath. "It was doing fine, but I had to move it because I lost my lease."

"Because you couldn't pay your bills?" he asked. "If you need money we can help you."

"But we think you should come back to work with us at Gray & Associates. That way you'll have a steady income," her mother said in a firm voice.

"Your mother is right. We're happy you reached for your dreams, but at some point, you need to realize that it's better to be practical. Look how well Graham's doing in the family business. Even Parker seems to be getting his life in order now."

Charlotte opened her mouth then shut it without saying anything. Her shoulders shook and she breathed raggedly. Luke couldn't take it anymore and stepped forward to address them.

"Your daughter is the best artist I've ever met. She must have something special if that gallery in Seattle wanted her for a solo show. She's also a talented businesswoman. Do you know how many people love her shop and visit it first thing when they come to Candle Beach?" Luke tried to keep his voice level but he wasn't winning the struggle.

Her father raised his eyebrows and her mother started to speak.

Luke held his finger in the air. "Wait. I'm not done. She doesn't need you telling her what to do. Who do you think organized this whole event? It wasn't me. I provided the barbecue, but she handled everything else—the marketing, the band, everything. She's a remarkable person and I'm proud of her for going after what she wants in life—even if *you* can't be happy for your own daughter."

During his tirade, Charlotte had been staring at him open-mouthed. By the time he finished, she'd turned a pretty shade of pink.

"Thank you, Luke." She shot him a small smile, then took a deep breath and turned to her parents. "He's right. I don't want to come back to work for Gray & Associates. I have my own business here and I'm going to be a successful artist. I'm confident in my abilities, even if you aren't." She stared at them pointedly and motioned in the direction of the parking area. "If you can't believe in me, please just go."

Her father spoke. "Honey, we didn't mean to make you think we don't believe in you. That's not the case...."

Luke slipped away as Charlotte and her parents talked. From what he'd heard, it was probably the most honest conversation the Gray family had ever had.

He walked with purpose toward the food truck. On the way, he passed Parker, who was assisting with cleanup.

"Hey," Parker said, clapping him on the back. "You did a great job with this event. Everyone loved it."

"Thanks. But it wasn't me. Charlotte put most of this together on her own." He glanced back to the barn, but couldn't see Charlotte or her parents from where he stood. He hoped they were treating her better now.

Parker whistled. "That explains how fantastic everything looks. She's always had a knack for design."

"Your parents don't seem to think she has a knack for anything," Luke said darkly.

Parker looked at him more closely. "What do you mean? I saw them here, but I haven't had a chance to talk with them. Are they still around?"

"Yeah. I just left them with Charlotte in the barn. She admitted to them that things weren't going perfectly in her life at the moment and they basically said 'I told you so' and tried to convince her that her place in the world is back working for them."

Parker's face blanched. "Ugh. Poor Charlotte. I've been on the receiving end of those types of conversations in the past as well, but I usually try to let it roll right off me. Nothing we ever do is good enough. Unfortunately, she tends to take things they say to her a little harder than I do."

"I'm not sure if I made things better or worse for her," he

admitted. "I may have slightly told them off." He shook his head. Had he really just done that? He wasn't sure whether his actions had endeared him to Charlotte or not.

Parker chuckled. "I would have loved to have seen that." He sobered. "How's she doing now?"

"I don't know. We're not on the best of terms right now so I didn't stay after I called out your parents for how they were treating her. When I left, it sounded like she was having a productive conversation with them. But she may still need some comforting later and I'm not the right person to do so."

His friend nodded. "Thanks for telling me. I'll go find them." He jetted off in the direction of the barn.

Luke watched him go. He would have liked to comfort Charlotte himself, but he didn't think they were in a place in their relationship where that would work. He missed her so much and had meant every word he said about her to her parents. It killed him to know that he'd had her and then lost her by being such an idiot—if only he'd handled the discussion over the lease better.

When Charlotte got back to the bookstore after the fundraiser ended, it was closed, but there was a light on in Dahlia's office. She wasn't sure she was in the mood to be social, but if Sarah was around, it wouldn't hurt to have a conversation with someone that wouldn't put her on edge. Plus, Sarah was a great listener and had comforted her when she'd come back after breaking up with Luke.

"Sarah? Is that you?" she called out.

"Yeah, hold on." A minute later, Sarah came out. "Sorry, I was trying to get some inventory numbers down before they all got mixed up. Dahlia left good instructions, but running a bookstore is more complicated than you'd think."

Charlotte smiled. "I know the feeling. I thought my to-do list was never going to end when I opened up Whimsical Delights."

"You look exhausted," Sarah said. "How was the event? Did you raise a lot of money?"

"I haven't tallied all of it up yet, but I think so. I'm too drained right now to do it tonight."

Sarah looked at her more closely. "Was it the event itself, or did something happen?"

"Wow, you're good." Charlotte peered at her. "How did you know it was something else?"

She shrugged. "As a teacher, you learn to read people— both students and parents. It comes in handy. I can tell immediately if a kid is lying to me. So, what's going on?"

"My parents were there."

"Oh. I take it you don't get along with them?"

"Yes and no. We get along, but our family has never been big on communicating. Also, they think that I can't be trusted to manage my own life."

"Ouch." Sarah winced. "I can't imagine."

"Yeah." Charlotte was quiet, unsure if she should say anything about Luke's monologue.

"Did you have a fight with them?"

Charlotte sighed. "They found out about the art show not going so well and having to move the trailer. Of course, that led them to believe that I should quit everything I want to do and come back to work for them." She paused. "Something happened though. Luke heard them talking down to me and gave them a tongue-lashing."

"Oh, wow." Sarah's eyes were wide. "He stood up for you."

Charlotte looked downward. "He did. He said the nicest things about me too." She met Sarah's gaze. "Was I wrong to give up on a relationship with him?"

Sarah hesitated, as if choosing her words wisely. "I think he hurt you, but perhaps he didn't mean to."

She thought about that. It was true that he didn't seem to understand why it was so hurtful for him to help her with financial situations—but that was a big part of the problem. She felt as though she'd told him several times how sensitive she was to interference in her finances and he'd still acted like it was nothing to subsidize her rent.

Still, talking to her parents today had made her realize the importance of communication. She'd finally made them realize how important her art was to her and that it wasn't something she planned to give up anytime soon. They'd seemed to understand and told her they wouldn't question her decision again. Having Luke tell them how proud he was of her seemed to have made them reconsider their stance.

He'd stood up for her, like no one ever had before. He hadn't come in to save her like some sort of white knight on a horse, but he'd helped her have the courage to talk to her parents honestly and given her confidence in her own abilities. She'd wanted to talk to him after the event, but by the time she finished, he was gone. Like Sarah said, maybe she should give him another chance.

"I suppose I could consider talking to him again. I'm scared though that if I let him back into my life, I'll fall into the trap of letting someone take care of me again. That's what happens every time I let my guard down with my parents."

"But Luke isn't your parents," Sarah said. "He cares

about you and wants the best for you. Do you really think he'll try to sabotage your independence?"

Charlotte stared at her. "No."

Was she more worried about her own reaction to him? That she'd want him to take care of her so she wouldn't have to work so hard? Luke had never been anything but nice to her and she'd shut him down. Did she doubt herself more than she doubted his intentions?

"Well then, that's your answer. If you still love him and don't think he's going to hurt you, why are you stalling when you could have a relationship with him?" Sarah sighed. "At this point, I'd give anything to have that opportunity. This town is way too small to throw away a relationship with a handsome, wealthy man who wants nothing more than to love you."

Charlotte smiled. "You're probably right." She stifled a yawn. "But I'm exhausted. I'll see you tomorrow, okay?"

"Goodnight," Sarah said. "I'll be finished here in a few minutes, but I'll try to not be too noisy."

Charlotte went upstairs, still thinking about Luke's interactions with her parents. It had been almost funny seeing her mother react to him. Not many people stood up to her. He had so many great qualities and everyone she knew seemed to think she should get back together with him, but a little part of her was still scared that she'd lose herself if she did.

It was late and she didn't want to think about it anymore. She got undressed and ready for bed, then laid her head down on the pillow, hoping to fall asleep immediately and have sweet dreams.

19

———

"You look awful," Parker said.

Luke scowled. "Thanks."

They'd met at the bowling alley in Haven Shores for a game after he'd closed the truck on Saturday night, but he was starting to regret accepting Parker's invitation.

"Have you been sleeping?"

"Some. Not enough."

"Is it still because of Charlotte?"

"Yeah."

Parker swore. "I knew it was a bad idea for the two of you to date. Now it's always going to be awkward when you're together."

"So sorry to inconvenience you. Wait, weren't you the one trying to convince me it was okay before? Ah, never mind. It hardly matters now."

Parker stared at him. "You really like her, don't you?"

Luke looked down at the table. "I think I love her. I mean, I know I do."

"You've got it bad. I've never seen you like this before."

"Unfortunately, she never wants to talk to me ever again."

"That sounds like something my sister would say." He chuckled. "She can be quite dramatic at times."

"Yeah." Luke rubbed his fingers over the frosty mug of beer.

"So, what are you going to do to win her back?"

"What do you mean?"

"Well, you can't give up on her so easily. You're obviously meant for each other. Besides, no one wants to see you moping around like this."

Luke felt his spirits rise. Was there a chance she'd take him back?

"I don't know. She's pretty mad at me."

"Not after you defended her from my parents. She was quite impressed."

"Really?" She hadn't said anything to him afterward, so he wasn't sure how to gage her reaction.

"Yeah. For the record, I was too. It's not easy to stand up to my mother." He laughed. "Believe me, I've been there."

"So, what can I do?"

Parker sipped his beer. "I don't know, but it had better be big. Can you think of anything she's mentioned that she wants?"

He thought about it. She wanted her half of the lot back, but he didn't think that would work. They couldn't get around the money issue with that and there was no way he was going to accidentally insult her ability to manage money again.

"I think I know what I want to do." He grinned at Parker. "Can you and Gretchen help?"

Parker clapped him on the back. "Anything you need."

~

"Dahlia." Charlotte embraced her friend. "I'm so glad you were able to be home in time for Maggie's wedding. How was your trip?"

They were standing in the freshly painted hallway outside of the master bedroom of the farmhouse at Sorensen Farm while Maggie changed into her wedding dress. Since Maggie wasn't having bridesmaids, they'd been allowed to wear whatever they wanted for the wedding. Charlotte wore the sundress she'd bought with Angel in Seattle, and Dahlia had dressed in an off-the-shoulder peach-colored dress that highlighted the tan she'd gained on her travels.

"Amazing." A far-off look came into Dahlia's eyes. "I can't believe how much we saw and yet how little we saw. There's so much to explore in Europe and I feel like we only touched the tip of it."

"I know. I've been to France and Italy, but I've always wanted to see everything else." Charlotte sighed. "I'm jealous that you got to go for over a month though."

"Well, I hear things have been pretty exciting for you too. You finally gave in and dated Parker's friend, right?"

Charlotte scrunched up her face and nodded.

"What happened between the two of you?" Dahlia leaned against the wall and folded her arms across her chest.

Charlotte gave her a sad smile. "I guess it just wasn't meant to be."

"Oh, come on, it's got to be more than that," Dahlia said. "I missed out on so much while I was gone."

"Are you saying you'd have rather stayed home?"

Dahlia laughed. "Well, no. But I do want to know what's going on with you. So, why did the two of you break up?"

Charlotte looked down at the white wedge sandals she'd pulled from the back of her closet. "He couldn't seem to understand that I want to make it on my own. There was a mix-up with the lot lease for Whimsical Delights and he ended up in control of the whole lot. I couldn't afford to pay him for half of it, and I didn't want to take any charity from him, so I had to move."

"Oh no." Dahlia peered at her. "That was such a great spot. Did you find something else?"

"I did, but it's nowhere near as nice as the old location."

Maggie opened the bedroom door, saving Charlotte from any more questions.

They gathered around her, oohing and aahing over her dress.

"Do you like it?" Maggie asked shyly, caressing the folds of the full white skirt with her fingertips.

"It's gorgeous," Charlotte said.

"Breathtaking," Dahlia agreed.

"Is she ready yet?" Gretchen called up the stairs.

"Yes!" they shouted.

Gretchen bounded up the steps, stopping behind Charlotte.

"Maggie, I love it."

Maggie beamed. "I didn't want or need a big wedding this time around, but I couldn't resist this dress. I saw it in the window of the bridal shop in Haven Shores when I was down there a few months ago." She twirled around. "Do you think Jake will like it?"

"Uh, yeah," Charlotte said. "He'd have to be crazy not to."

Gretchen checked her watch. "Everyone's ready in the barn. It's showtime."

They helped Maggie with her dress as they walked from the house to the barn, and then they slipped into the barn ahead of her, taking their seats. Jake stood at the front of the room with only a minister, looking nervous. Maggie had wanted a small wedding, so only her close family and friends were there, occupying two rows of white wooden chairs situated on either side of a main aisle.

Charlotte peeked behind her to see if Maggie was ready. She appeared in the doorway and nodded to Gretchen, who hit a button on the CD player, sending the first notes of Pachelbel's Canon throughout the room. Charlotte turned to watch Jake's face as his future wife approached. His chest had puffed out and a calm look had come over his face as he watched Maggie come down the aisle. This was clearly a man who was marrying the woman he loved.

They joined at the front and the minister had them recite their vows, then Maggie's son Alex came forward with the rings. They slipped the rings on the other's fingers and Jake pulled Maggie close for a long kiss.

All of the wedding guests cheered, and Charlotte noticed tears in the eyes of Jake's mother. This must have been a bittersweet moment for her as she watched the widow of her younger son, Brian, marrying her older son Jake. It was clear to everyone though that even though it had come about through a sad situation, Maggie and Jake belonged together now. Alex came up to the front again and they wrapped their arms around him, Maggie kissing him on the top of his head before they all looked up and smiled for their family and friends.

The three of them walked back down the aisle to the back of the barn, which had been pre-set with a few round tables and a rectangular table for a buffet. Everyone else followed Maggie and Jake, congratulating them. Jake's mom gave her an especially big hug.

Charlotte swallowed a lump in her throat. The way that Jake looked at Maggie, the way that he genuinely adored Alex—that was what she wanted. A man who'd be there for her, no matter what happened.

They filled their plates with food and sat down around the tables, with Charlotte sitting next to Alex, who was the only other single person at the wedding, and he was a child. Maggie's parents, Jake's parents, Dahlia and Garrett, Gretchen and Parker, Angel and Adam—everyone had found their perfect match.

She pressed her lips together to keep from breaking out into tears and leaned over to address Alex. "You're going to dance with me, right?"

His eyes widened, as if he wasn't sure if she was for real. His expression was priceless, and almost made being the lone single adult worth it. Almost, but not quite.

"I'm joking," she said. "Don't worry. You don't have to dance with me."

"Oh, okay, good." He dug into the plate of food that his grandmother had brought him.

Charlotte chose not to take his rejection personally and bit into a delicately formed beef Wellington, the crust melting in her mouth.

"Did you make this?" she asked Angel, who was seated on her left side.

Angel nodded. "I had help with the filling, but the rest of it I made myself. Maggie wanted me to make something new for her wedding. Do you like it?"

"Uh, yeah. It's pretty much the best thing I've ever eaten."

"Thanks." Angel blushed. "How are you doing? If you don't mind me saying so, I know these kinds of things can be rough without a date."

Charlotte stared at the food on her plate. "I'm fine."

"You miss him, don't you," Angel observed. "You've been miserable ever since you two broke up."

"I know, but that doesn't mean we were meant to be together. We can't all be like Maggie and Jake."

"No, but you also don't want to throw away something that could be special. Maybe give him another chance?"

"Maybe." By now, she really didn't know what to think. All she knew was that all she could think about was Luke and how he made her feel like she was special and could accomplish anything. How many men would stand up to her parents like he had? But did he really think she could make it on her own, or was he just like her parents? She stood from the table and excused herself.

By this time, music was playing out of overhead speakers and couples were moving onto the dance floor. Jake and Maggie waltzed by in each other's arms and Charlotte's stomach began to hurt.

"Do you want to dance?" a familiar voice asked.

Charlotte smiled and turned to Parker. "I'd love that, thank you."

Her brother held out his hands. "I get to lead this time."

She laughed. When they were kids, they'd always fought over who got to lead—probably a function of being the youngest kids in the family, who never came out on top of anything.

"Just this once."

They danced together for a few songs, chatting amicably.

"Doesn't Gretchen mind you dancing with me?"

"Nope, she suggested it actually." He quickly added, "Not that I mind dancing with you."

"Uh-huh."

"You know, Luke really misses you."

She was quiet, not sure where her brother was going with this.

"Charlotte, seriously. The guy is miserable without you. Isn't there any way you'd consider taking him back?" He shook his head. "I've never seen him like this before. He's a mess."

"He looked fine at the fundraiser." He had seemed more subdued than normal, but she'd chalked that up to him being polite to her. Thinking about the fundraiser and being in the barn again brought back memories of him defending her to her parents.

Luke had been like a white knight, trying to save her from her dragon parents. His actions could be construed as stepping in to save her when she couldn't do it herself, but she didn't think that had been his intention. In fact, he'd appeared to be genuinely surprised with himself that he'd told her parents off.

She grinned. They hadn't known what to think, but when she'd continued talking to them after Luke left, they'd begun to understand things from her perspective. His outburst had resulted in the first real talk she'd had with them since she'd left for college.

"Yeah, well, he's not."

Gretchen came up to Parker and put her hand on his shoulder. "How are things going?"

He smiled at her. "I'm trying to tell her how she's devastated my best friend."

"Ah." Gretchen regarded him knowingly and then looked at Charlotte. "Any chance you'll forgive Luke? We had him over for dinner last night and he was really down."

Although she knew they meant well, she felt like she was being steamrolled by her friends.

"I'm not feeling well. I think I'm going to head out." She gave them a small smile and hoped that they wouldn't ask her any more questions.

"Oh." Gretchen snapped her fingers. "I completely forgot to tell you. I was driving past your shop on the way here and the lights were still on."

"What? I swear I turned them off before I left." She'd closed the shop early today to get ready for Maggie's wedding and may have forgotten because of her excitement about it. "Oh well, I can swing by on my way home. Thanks for letting me know." She gave them both small hugs and glanced at Maggie, who was beaming and deep in conversation with her in-laws. "Can you please tell Maggie I had to go? I don't want to interrupt her right now."

They nodded.

"Sure," Gretchen said.

Charlotte waved at some of her other friends as she walked out, not wanting to get into her reasons for leaving with all of them too. She walked out into the cool air and got into her car, where she finally allowed herself a moment to cry. When she felt better, she inserted her keys into the ignition and drove back to town.

20

*W*hen she reached Candle Beach's downtown area, she parked her car where she usually did near her apartment. It was a nice night so she decided to walk from there to Whimsical Delights to check on the trailer in the new lot.

The town was fairly quiet at ten o'clock on a Sunday night and she only passed one other person on her way to the shop. When she neared it, she did a double take. Gretchen had been right—there were lights on in the shop —and fairy lights strung up on the old fence, which she hadn't put there. What was going on?

Her favorite easy-listening song suddenly filled the air. This had to be some weird dream. She moved closer to the trailer, still not understanding.

From behind the Airstream, Luke stepped out, carrying a bouquet of red roses.

She looked up at him. "What are you doing here?" She motioned to the lot. "And what's going on?"

He handed her the bouquet, which she took from him

without thinking. The scent of the roses teased her nostrils and she breathed deeply. They'd always been her favorites.

"I wanted to apologize and beg for you to take me back," he said.

Her head shot up from the bouquet. "Did you do all of this?"

He nodded. "Well, I had some help. Parker and Gretchen came here to help me as soon as you left this afternoon."

Her mouth gaped open. "They were in on it too?" Well, that explained the looks they'd exchanged when they were trying to entice her to check on her trailer.

Not that it hadn't worked. She looked around. The rickety old fence was straighter and bore a fresh coat of white paint. Luke had strung twinkly white lights up on the top of it, and stretched the string of lights across to her trailer. A new wrought iron patio table and matching chairs was situated next to the trailer, on a new bed of crushed oyster shells. Even the straggly rose bush in the corner had received a facelift and a supportive white trellis to lean on. And—how had she not noticed it before?—someone had set up a tall white platform surrounded by white latticework behind her trailer.

She walked over to it, looking up. "It's like a hunting blind. But why is it here?"

He grinned. "Yep." He moved closer to it and motioned to the ladder. "I had someone build it and bring it out here for you."

"I don't understand. Why do I need a hunting blind?"

"It's actually an artist's loft for you. If you sit on the platform, you can get a great view of the ocean."

Her eyes widened. "Really?" She climbed the ladder to the top, her hands easily gripping the smooth metal rungs. The deck was about eight feet by eight feet and sat a few feet above the roof of the Airstream. Luke was right—it offered a fantastic view. Tears filled her eyes.

"Do you like it?" he called up.

She looked over the edge at him, tears streaming down her cheeks. "I love it. Thank you."

"But you're crying." Concern was etched across his face.

"They're happy tears." She sat upright and wiped her face, then surveyed the lot. In the space of a few hours, he'd transformed the place. She'd never dreamed it could be this beautiful.

"Okay. Uh, are you coming back down?"

"Right now." She climbed down and ran into his arms. "Thank you."

He enveloped her in a huge hug. "You're welcome. And Charlotte, I'm so sorry. I never meant to offend you or anything. I know you can make it on your own. I never once doubted that."

He may not have, but she had doubted herself, and his support had made all the difference when she spoke with her parents.

"I know." Her words were muffled against his chest and her tears of joy wetted his shirt.

"So why are you still crying?" He traced the tips of his fingers lightly across her back and she finally tipped her head back to look up at him.

"I don't know." She continued to sob. All the emotions she'd experienced over the last few months were hitting her full blast—sadness, excitement, joy, and now this—pure love for another person like she'd never felt before.

"This is amazing," she said finally. "I love that you did this for me. And I love you."

A wide smile spread across his face. "I love you too." He reached up, hooking a curled finger under her chin and lifting her face to him as he leaned down to meet her mouth. She no longer noticed the wetness of her cheeks and eyes. A pulsating warmth started in her chest, radiating out to the rest of her body and bringing a flush to her face. He kissed her deeply, but gently. She pulled tightly against his back in an effort to be closer to him, never wanting to let him go. She remained lost in the kiss until she was light-headed and tingly. When their lips finally parted, she was completely breathless. They remained in each other's arms for a bit, and Charlotte gazed up at him lovingly.

She sighed and rested her head against him, contentedly listening to his heart beating. It had taken them over a decade and a fresh start in Candle Beach to realize they were meant for each other, but now, she was never going to let him go.

21

*T*wo long tables flanked by folding chairs had been set up in the parking lot next to Charlotte's Airstream trailer. The night was perfect—balmy, with a slight breeze.

Charlotte checked her watch and said to Luke, "They should be here soon."

As if on cue, their friends started to arrive, each carrying a dish for the potluck. Luke had placed an ice chest in the shade, and the men disappeared behind the platform to dig in it for beers as soon as they arrived.

"I told you that this could look nice," Gretchen said as she placed a bowl full of Swedish meatballs on the table. "I love the little lights and the oyster shells. You've done a nice job with the space."

"Thanks." Charlotte smiled. "But that was all Luke."

"What's with the platform?" Angel asked. "I like the white latticework on it, but I can't figure out what it's for."

"Luke had it built for me so that I can go up there and paint. From that height, I can see the ocean." A warmth spread throughout her body. It still amazed her how thoughtful he'd been. Perching on top of the Airstream had been okay, but having the space on top of the platform to spread out while she worked was wonderful.

Gretchen lifted an eyebrow. "Wow, when Parker told him to come up with something big to show you how much he loves you, he really went all out."

"Yeah. About that—what's with you and Parker getting involved in my love life?" Charlotte mock-glared at Gretchen.

Gretchen laughed. "Well, somebody had to. The two of you weren't doing too well on your own."

Charlotte narrowed her eyes at Gretchen. "I'll remember that next time you two get in some silly argument."

Maggie rolled her eyes at them. "Seriously? You guys are as bad as sisters."

"You'd have been in on it too if it hadn't been your wedding we used to keep her occupied." Gretchen grinned.

"Okay, okay." Dahlia poured herself a glass of white wine. "I'm just glad everything worked out between the two of you."

"Yeah, I was rooting for you, even if you did go after the man you'd promised to set me up with." Sarah sighed dramatically. "Now where am I going to find someone?"

"Oh, I'm sure we can think of someone," Dahlia said.

"Yeah, if you want us to do some matchmaking, I'm sure we can fix you up with a nice guy." Maggie winked at her.

Sarah wrinkled her face up. "I'm not big on blind dates or matchmaking. I mean, Charlotte was going to fix me up with this tall, handsome, single guy she knew, and instead she took him for herself." She looked at Charlotte, who blushed.

"Sorry about that," Charlotte said. "I swear I didn't know that I liked him then."

"Hey, what's going on over here?" Garrett asked. "What's this I hear about matchmaking?"

"Nothing," Sarah said, her face turning the same shade as the beets Maggie had brought. "Just some overeager friends of mine that think I should be as happily coupled as they all are."

Garrett put his arm around Dahlia. "And what's wrong with that?" He gave his wife a big kiss on the lips and she jabbed him in the side, while smiling at him.

Adam appeared, eating a miniature apple tart.

"Adam!" Angel admonished him. "Those were for dessert."

He looked at it sheepishly. "Isn't it always dessert time?"

She sighed. "We should probably eat before Adam devours all of the treats I brought."

Adam swallowed a piece of apple. "I couldn't help myself. These are delicious."

"That's what I told her," Maggie said. "I said she should really open up a bakery in town. I'd miss her at the café, but her talents aren't showcased enough there."

Angel looked down at the ground.

"That would be fantastic," Charlotte said. "I'd be there every day. You have to do it."

"I'm thinking about it," Angel mumbled.

Adam finished his tart and wrapped his arm around her waist. "I'm trying to talk her into it."

"But Maggie has so much to do at the café," Angel said.

"She can hire someone to help, just like I did at the bookstore," Dahlia said. "That's worked out wonderfully and I made a new friend in the process."

"I just hope I can work some of the weekends once school starts, but I'll help out for sure during school breaks. It's been fun to see adults on a regular basis." Sarah motioned to Adam. "I think my brother is about to eat the tablecloth. Maybe we should eat now."

It was Adam's turn to glare now. Charlotte laughed. It was interesting to see the dynamics between the siblings and she wondered if she and Parker provided as much entertainment for their friends as Adam and Sarah did.

Jake led Maggie over to the far end of the table, and the others followed suit.

Charlotte's eyes roved over the offerings, her mouth watering at the sight of Luke's barbecued chicken. "It's like Thanksgiving in July."

Luke came up behind her and placed his hands on her shoulders. "It is, and I'm thankful to have come to Candle Beach and be spending this evening with you and our friends."

After everyone left, Charlotte and Luke cleaned up the stray dishes and set them in a tub to take home to wash. She looked around the lot. It was difficult to see that this was the same empty dirt lot that she'd toured with Gretchen. She'd been blinded by fear and sadness then, but now she could see its potential. Even the construction across the road hadn't been that noisy so far and her repeat customers seemed to have found her new location.

"That went well, I think," Luke said as he picked up a wine glass that had been left on the long dining table.

"I think so." Charlotte folded the white linen tablecloth and put it on a side table before folding up the long table. "We should do this more often."

"I agree." They finished the cleanup and packed everything into Charlotte's car.

"Do you want to watch the sunset with me from your artist's loft?" He jutted his thumb upward.

"Sure." She climbed up the ladder in front of him and sat down on the platform while gazing out at the ocean. "Wow. I'll never get tired of this." Her fingers itched to sketch it.

"You'd rather be painting than be with me, huh?" he teased her as he sat down next to her.

"Wrong," she said, leaning over to kiss him squarely on the mouth. "I'd rather be painting up here *with* you."

She pulled a sketchbook out of the plastic drawers she'd stored up in the loft and folded the used pages over. "Stay right there." She quickly drew his features with the outlines of the sun setting behind him, then set her drawing down.

"All done?" he asked.

She scooted closer until she was facing him. "Thank you."

"For what?" he asked

"For this loft, the decorating you did, for being you, and for believing in me." She punctuated each item with a light kiss. When she was done, he pulled her close, not letting her go.

They sat on the platform, watching the sun set over the ocean. They may have taken a rocky path to end up where they were now, but she wouldn't have changed it for anything. Together, they had history, and she couldn't imagine anyone she'd rather share her future with than Luke.

Thank you for reading SWEET HISTORY! If you enjoyed it, please leave a review on Amazon.

Did you miss any of the other Candle Beach books?
    Book #1: Dahlia's story — Sweet Beginnings
    Book #2: Gretchen's story — Sweet Success
    Book #3: Maggie's story — Sweet Promises
    Book #4: Angel's story — Sweet Memories

Also by Nicole Ellis
    Jill Andrews Cozy Mysteries

AVAILABLE ON AMAZON AND KINDLE UNLIMITED

<<<<>>>>